Beyond Stonebridge

by

Linda Griffin

A sequel to Stonebridge

The Wild Rose Press, Inc.
PO Box 708
Adams Basin, NY 14410-0708
Visit us at www.thewildrosepress.com

Publishing History
First Edition, 2024
Trade Paperback ISBN 978-1-5092-5427-9
Digital ISBN 978-1-5092-5428-6

A sequel to Stonebridge
Published in the United States of America

Dedication

To William and Darryl, who gave me Ted

Acknowledgments

Thanks are owed to Judith Walzer Leavitt for her book *Make Room for Daddy: The Journey from Waiting Room to Birthing Room* and, as always, to my wonderful editor, Nan Swanson.

Chapter One

Stonebridge Manor, Brenford County, Virginia
August 1959

Sgt. Chandler paced thoughtfully across the sitting room rug. He was a thin, tense young man, filled with nervous energy, and he didn't believe anything he was being told.

Ted sighed. "It was an accident, Sergeant," he said again.

"A suspicious accident."

"Yes," Ted said. He was sitting sideways on the damask-covered sofa with a pillow under his left leg and an ice bag on the knee.

Sgt. Chandler pivoted at the far end of the beautifully paneled room. "But you admit a fight took place?"

"We had a fight. Yes."

"And…?"

"I didn't kill him. We fought, yes, but I wouldn't have killed him."

Rynna raised her head. Wouldn't he? The struggle had been in deadly earnest. She was as jumpy as Sgt. Chandler and not much happier with their account. If they told him Jason had seen a ghost, he wouldn't believe it. The omission left a large hole in the story.

Her handsome young husband, the father of her

1

unborn child, was dead. Stonebridge, the elegant Georgian manor she had come to live in over a year ago, was now a crime scene. Two sober men from the coroner's office had shrouded Jason's body and carried it away on a stretcher, but a chalk outline remained in the hall where he had fallen. Ted's wheelchair still lay on its side at the top of the stairs, where Jason had stumbled over it. The police had taken measurements and made chalk marks where Jason must have stood to put a bullet in the wall. Another bullet hole was in the ceiling, where he had fired above Ted's head. Their story explained that one. The one in the wall troubled Sgt. Chandler.

"Did the gun discharge when he fell?" he asked.

"No," Ted said with resigned patience. "He fired first."

"Why?" the detective demanded. "You were by the railing, behind him. Mrs. Wyatt—"

"Rynna," she corrected. She didn't want to be called Mrs. Wyatt anymore.

"Rynna, then. You were—"

Ted interrupted him. "Sergeant, the man wasn't behaving rationally. What can I tell you?"

"He tried to push Ted down the stairs," Rynna said. She had said little except under direct questioning, but she was tired of all this. Jason was dead, and they couldn't change that brutal fact.

Sgt. Chandler left the puzzling bullet hole and returned to the fight. They hadn't changed a word of their story, and their separate versions matched in every important detail. He would have been inclined to believe them if Jason's mysterious death had been the first in this house. "Mr. Wyatt has contusions on his throat," he said, beginning to pace again, "which are consistent with having been choked."

"So do I," she said. "And Ted…" She rose from the straight-backed armchair where she had sat passively for the last twenty minutes and walked to the sofa. Ted gazed at her gravely, and she tugged open his collar to show the marks on his neck.

"Yes," Sgt. Chandler acknowledged. Jason had given as much as he'd received. "He also has strange bruises on his legs," he added.

"Where I slammed into him with the wheelchair," Ted said. He would be glad to demonstrate the maneuver when they finished with their chalk lines and measuring tapes. He was all right—he could handle Sgt. Chandler's questions, and his injured knee didn't concern him—but he was a little impatient.

"I suppose you know I'm not satisfied," Sgt. Chandler said.

"Yes," Ted said. Chandler wasn't likely to be satisfied, not as long as they couldn't tell the whole story. "I suppose you still think I killed my great-grandmother."

Sgt. Chandler didn't answer. "Wyatt was crazy, jealous," he mused, almost to himself. He glanced at Rynna and asked, "Did he have reason?"

She kept her gaze steady. "He never needed a reason."

Chandler snapped his little notebook shut. "All right, that's enough for now. I'll let you folks get some sleep. I'll be back, though, probably tomorrow."

"Is it all right to move the wheelchair?" Ted asked.

"Sorry, yes. Leave the chalk. We'll clean it up when we're finished. Good night."

Rynna accompanied him to the door. When she

returned, she sat on the edge of the armchair and gazed at Ted. What could she say? Jason was between them even more than when he was alive.

"Why don't you go to bed?" he asked.

She shook her head. "I'll wait until Dr. Moran comes. I won't sleep anyway." She got to her feet again and paced restlessly around the room, aware of Ted's watchful eyes.

"Rynna," he said tentatively.

She faced him. "You're glad he's dead, aren't you?"

"No," he said at once, genuinely shocked.

"It's what you wanted, isn't it? You wanted him out of the way."

"Is he out of the way?"

She shook her head. "I'm sorry." She didn't mean to attack him. She was confused and frightened. Her husband was dead, but the knot in the pit of her stomach was for Ted. Her concern drew her back to the sofa. A half hour ago he had been sick from pain and shock and now he was relieved and shaky, his color much better. He was almost euphoric because they had both survived. His pain was proof they had lived through the ordeal.

"Hey," he said, holding out his hand. He needed a minute to figure out what she was upset about. He linked his fingers with hers and asked, teasing, "What's the matter? Are you afraid I'll be crippled for life?" Since he was already disabled by arthritis, the damage Jason had inflicted was insignificant. "Hey," he said again when she didn't smile at his joke. "It's okay, Rynna. It's nothing."

"It isn't nothing," she insisted. His casual attitude about serious things could be infuriating, but it was also part of what she loved about him. "You would probably laugh if *I* had an injured knee," she suggested.

"Your legs are prettier than mine," he said.

"It's not funny, Ted. Jason is dead."

"Yes," he said soberly. She sat gingerly on the edge of the sofa, careful not to jostle him, and he put his arm around her awkwardly. "Cry if you want to," he said. A generous offer—he would hate it if she did.

"*Are* you glad he's dead?" she asked.

"I'm glad we aren't."

"Did you think he was going to kill us?"

He didn't answer. Brisk footsteps approached, and Rynna rose from the sofa. Discretion was still called for.

Lucy, tearstained and subdued, announced, "Dr. Moran is here."

"Thank you, Lucy. Send him in." She turned to Ted, relieved.

"Go to bed now," he said.

"No, I want to stay. I want to hear what he says."

"I don't want you in here making a fuss."

"I won't," she began, but he wouldn't give in, and she backed away. "Ted," she said quickly, hearing Dr. Moran's steps outside the door, her heart skipping a beat. This was more dangerous than ever. "I love you."

He let her stay.

"My dear Mrs. Wyatt," the white-haired physician said. He set his medical bag on the end table and grasped her hands. "This is most distressing. Such a terrible accident." His kind brown eyes were sincerely sympathetic.

"Yes," Rynna murmured. She hoped she wouldn't have to face too much of this—the condolences of people who never knew the real Jason.

"Would you like something to help you sleep

tonight? A mild sedative, nothing that would affect the baby."

"No," she said. "Nothing, thank you. Just look at Ted's knee, please."

"Of course." He picked up his bag and shifted a chair over beside the sofa.

Rynna started to tell him what had happened, and Ted said, "Rynna, sit down and shut up." She sat. Tonight, she had seen a ghost, had seen her husband fall to his death. Nothing else would faze her.

Dr. Moran set aside the ice bag and said, "Hmm," in his best professional manner. "Considerable swelling. Hard to tell." He took Ted's wrist to gauge his pulse. "How are you feeling generally?"

"Fine."

"You look like hell. Do you feel cold? Nauseated?"

"No."

"He was earlier," Rynna put in. Ted gave her a stern look.

Dr. Moran retrieved a long needle and a small bottle from his bag. While he waited for the anesthetic to take effect, he said, "It looks as if somebody kicked you in the shin, as well."

"Somebody did."

"Is that right?" the physician said, as if he didn't believe it. He ran his hand over the bruises and said, "Hmm," again. After a moment he touched Ted's knee and asked, "Do you feel this?"

"No."

"Good." He probed with expert fingers, assessing the damage. "It doesn't seem too serious, but I'd like to be sure. How about coming to the hospital tomorrow for an x-ray?"

"I don't think so."

Dr. Moran wasn't surprised. "We'll see how it is tomorrow," he said. He replaced the ice bag and got to his feet, and Rynna rose too.

"Thank you," she said, holding out her hand.

He studied her for a minute. "Go to bed. Try to get some sleep." To Ted he said, "I'm not going to tell you to stay in bed tomorrow, because you won't do it anyway, but stay off that leg. Do us both a favor."

"I'll see that he does," Rynna promised.

Ted threw discretion to the winds. "I'm crazy about this woman, Phil," he said. "She keeps trying to run my life, but she's a real Demeray."

Rynna was astonished. Dr. Moran took it in stride. "Good night," he said, smiling. He saw himself out, and Rynna stared at Ted. *I'm crazy about this woman...She's a real Demeray.* Roughly translated: I love you too.

****

She slept badly. Twice she dreamed Jason was hitting and choking her and woke up crying. The second time she lay still in the darkness, shivering with cold and very much alone.

She couldn't deny the truth. She was glad he was dead.

****

In the morning, she had a lot to think about, matters she could deal with in a practical way, but she had no sense of connection with any of these things. Widow was only a word. She had so many details to handle, funeral arrangements, people she had to notify. They wouldn't hear the whole story, not from her. Jason was dead. That was enough.

She didn't see Ted at breakfast in the dining room

and hoped he was sleeping late. She listlessly ate bland-tasting oatmeal and sipped steaming tea for the baby's sake but couldn't manage more than a few bites of buttery biscuit. When Lucy told her Ted was up, she climbed the stairs to his austere room and found him cleaning out his desk drawers, packing to move out as planned.

"Ted," she said. "You are impossible."

"Good morning."

"Dr. Moran said you should stay in bed."

"No, he didn't. He said to stay off of it, which I am doing. I wish you'd stop fussing. I told you it was all right."

"You wouldn't tell me if it wasn't. Why do you have to do that now?"

"I think it would be best if I'm out of here tonight."

"There's no hurry, is there? Everything has changed. You can stay."

"No, I can't."

"I don't want to be alone here."

"You won't be alone. The servants are here."

"But…"

"Rynna, think. There'll be a scandal. Whatever the police can or cannot prove, nobody is going to believe we're entirely innocent."

"I don't care what they think. I don't believe you do either."

He shrugged. "Nevertheless…"

"Are you afraid to stay here with me?"

"You *are* a dangerous woman." He closed a drawer for emphasis.

Rynna was in no mood for this. "We'll talk later," she said. At the door she looked back. "Ted…did we kill him?" If they hadn't been together—just talking, but together—in Ted's room, if Jason hadn't found them together…

"No. It happened, that's all. It's over."

Yes, he looked at life that way. What was over was over.

But was it?

****

Dr. Moran returned after lunch and spent a few minutes with Rynna in the sitting room before he checked on Ted. She admitted she hadn't slept well, and he gave her some pills she didn't intend to take. He took her blood pressure, listened to the baby's heart, and said she would be fine. "The Demerays are tough," he said.

He was upstairs for a long time and said only, "Don't worry."

Sgt. Chandler came back with typed statements for them to sign. They sat in the spacious dining room over coffee, and he asked some of the same questions again and a few new ones.

"Mrs. Wyatt—"

"Please call me Rynna."

"Yesterday you said…" He consulted his notebook. "Wyatt was insanely jealous."

"I don't think I said insanely."

"Sorry. He was always accusing you of infidelity, et cetera, 'He never needed a reason.' But did he have one?" She didn't know what to say. The memory of stolen kisses in the music room was now as remote as her early happiness with Jason.

Ted answered for her. "We haven't broken the seventh commandment, Sgt. Chandler. Nor the sixth."

Rynna didn't know whether the detective was

convinced of anything, but she was impressed. Ted was pretty good in the clutch. It was technically true. They hadn't committed adultery, and they hadn't killed Jason. Whether Ted had coveted his cousin's wife was a different matter.

After Sgt. Chandler left, they sat together in silence. Rynna didn't know what Ted was thinking. Whatever level of intimacy they had attained, dangerous as it had been, was now gone. She was tired and discouraged. Was he sorry their relationship had ever begun? Was it all over? The results had been deadly.

"What are you thinking?" he asked.

She had no answer, nothing she could've admitted. "Ted, please stay tonight," she said instead.

He shook his head. "I think we need the time apart."

"Do we?"

He drummed his fingers lightly on the table. "I do."

That was clear enough. He didn't want to be under the same roof with her. "All right," she said. Was he forgetting how recently she had been trying to get him to *leave*? They had changed sides. Until a few days ago she'd wanted him out, and he hadn't wanted to leave her alone—with Jason. "Are you angry with me?" she asked.

He shook his head. But now, when she needed him most, he was leaving her. "Please don't cry," he said.

"I'm not." She was, but she kept her head bowed so he wouldn't see. She blinked back the tears and took a sip of tepid coffee. "All right," she said steadily enough. "Do what you like." She raised her head, the danger of tears past. "Do me a favor, will you?"

"What?"

"Get a haircut. I don't want you to look shaggy at the funeral."

****

Not long after Ted and Ellery, the chauffeur, loaded the Bentley with boxes and drove into town, Rynna received another blow. Cecile, who had been her only friend in the early days of her life at Stonebridge, came to her with downcast eyes and gave notice. With a small shock of despair, Rynna realized Cecile thought she and Ted were responsible for Jason's death. Maybe all the servants did.

Stonebridge was beginning to resemble the proverbial sinking ship. Ellery would leave soon too, for a better opportunity, one he had been considering even before his recent quarrel with Jason. She was sad about losing him too, knowing he and Ted had been friends for many years.

Maybe she should leave. Stonebridge was only recently her home. She had no real ties here. She could find better places to raise a child. She could sell the house. The Demeray family had owned the estate for centuries, but it was hers to dispose of. Would Grandmother forgive her? Would Ted?

She slept a little better than she had the first night, even though she felt more alone than ever. Ted was so far way, sleeping tonight in the attractive apartment on the edge of the university campus. They had checked it out together—how many days ago? He had said he would always see her standing at the window, gazing out at the view. Did he think of her tonight? Did she want him to? Should they try to find their way back?

****

In the morning she awoke filled with dread, sensing a cloud hanging over her future. What she remembered first was not Jason's death but her estrangement from

Ted.

She was in the cheerful yellow nursery, aimlessly fussing with the new animal-patterned curtains, when Lucy told her she had a phone call. "Thank you, Lucy," she said listlessly. "I'll take it in the bedroom. Who is it, do you know?"

"Yes, ma'am. It's Mr. Demeray."

Mr. Demeray, she thought stupidly. My Mr. Demeray? She was shocked to realize she had never talked to him on the telephone. This was the first time they had been apart, except for her honeymoon with Jason, since she moved to Stonebridge more than a year ago. A thousand things like this, utterly commonplace, had never come up in the sheltered world of Stonebridge.

She picked up the extension in the master bedroom. "Ted?"

"Yes. Good morning." He sounded perfectly natural.

"Good morning. Do you know we've never talked on the phone before?"

"No, of course not," he said. "How are you?"

"I'm all right. Cecile is leaving."

"Cecile? I'm sorry. She…"

"Yes. She always admired Jason." An awkward silence followed. Rynna was disoriented, as if she had never used a telephone in her life. "Did you sleep all right?" she asked. "Is the apartment…?"

"It's fine." Silence again. Why was conversation so difficult? Why did he call if he had nothing to say?

"Ted…"

"Before I forget, let me give you the number here. In case you need to get in touch with me. Do you have a pencil?"

"Of course not. I'll try to remember it."

He gave her the number. Was that why he had called? "Can you remember that?"

"Yes, I think so."

"I know you have things to do," he said. "I won't keep you."

"No, I—"

"I just called to— When I left yesterday, I forgot to tell you…"

"Yes, what?" she asked. Had he left some of his books or papers behind or some minor task undone?

"I love you," he said and hung up.

Chapter Two

A great many people were at the funeral, unlike the small, subdued group at Grandmother's service in the same little stone church. Rynna didn't know more than a handful of them, Jason's closest friends and colleagues. In addition, other lawyers she had never met, a judge, and a few grateful clients were in attendance. Much to her surprise, even reporters and two discreetly watchful police officers showed up. Jason had been charming, well-liked, and successful. In death he was also a minor celebrity—*Young Lawyer Dies in Tragic Fall.*

She and Ted were the only family left on Jason's mother's side, but his cousin Ian Wyatt came all the way from Vermont. He had been kind to her when she was a new bride spending Christmas with his family. Janet and the children hadn't come, but he said they sent their love. He was the only person at the funeral, besides Ted, who didn't stare at her, speculating as to whether or not she'd killed her husband.

When the graveside service was over, Ian took her arm. He was puzzled as well as bereaved. "Can you tell me what happened?" he asked.

"I'll try." She took him to meet Ted, who was exchanging a few words with Cy Harris. "I'll see you at the house later," she said. "I want to talk to Ian."

They strolled up the hill, and Rynna was overtaken by a bitter memory of standing here with Jason at

Grandmother's funeral. She'd wanted to examine the stones in the family plot because she hadn't been in the cemetery before, but he'd been edgy and impatient. She took her time now, stopping at each familiar name, the Hutchinsons and the Demerays who had lived at Stonebridge for centuries.

"Jason was ill," she told Ian. "He needed professional help, but he wouldn't go. You know how proud he was."

"He was fine at Christmas."

"Yes, he was. Most of the time he was. But he…" She moved on, keeping her gaze on the gravestones.

"Tell me, Rynna." He was skeptical, but willing to listen.

"He's dead. It doesn't seem fair now." She stopped and turned to meet his eyes. "At times I hated him. I even wished him dead. But he couldn't help it. It isn't fair to blame him now if he was mentally ill."

"Are you telling me Jason beat you?"

"Yes."

"That's hard to believe."

"Yes, I know it is. It was hard to believe when it was happening to me. But it kept happening. He hit me, choked me, raped me." She unbuttoned the collar of her ugly black dress and showed him the fading bruises on her throat. "Once he—"

"My God," he said. "Just like Uncle Alex."

"Yes," she said, grateful he had said it first.

"I'm sorry," he said. "I wish I'd known. I might have been able to do something."

"I don't think so, but thank you, Ian." They ambled on a bit, silent but close in understanding. A little farther on, where she would've found it months ago, if Jason hadn't rushed her away, was a small, weathered gravestone.

To the Memory of William Charles Demeray, Jr.
Dearly Beloved Son of William and Clara
Suffer the Little Children to Come unto Me.

Ted's brother, although the word was a strange one to use. The infant whose death had led to his adoption. If she had seen the stone the day of Grandmother's funeral, she would have asked Ted for an explanation, and then what? She was already engaged to Jason and deeply in love with him. She wouldn't have been as vulnerable as she was later, after her marriage began to fall apart. She wouldn't have experienced such a sudden emotional upheaval. But was that love?

Suffer the little children to come unto me. How brave of Clara to face her loss with such faith. Rynna couldn't have gone on, as Clara had with Ted, without overprotecting the second child.

Ian, to whom the names meant nothing, said, "That's the saddest thing of all, to bury a child."

They drifted on, and she said, "Ian, I wanted to tell you something else. I haven't talked about it with anyone, not even Ted, and he was there. We didn't tell the police. You'll understand why."

"What?" He was immediately alarmed.

"Ever since I came to Stonebridge," she began, "I've sometimes felt a presence in the house."

"Are you saying it's haunted?" He was ready to be amused.

"No, I wouldn't call it that. I'm sure you don't want to hear all the details now, but from the beginning I believed it was Rosalind, Jason's mother…in some way a renewal of her spirit."

He backed away. "I know you must be upset."

"No, please listen. The night Jason died, I saw her. We all did. That's why he—"

"For God's sake," Ian said roughly. "You think *he* needed help?"

"I did see her, and so did Ted."

He didn't believe her, and he was angry with her for believing what she had seen with her own eyes. She didn't hear everything he said, and when he went back down the hill to his rented car, she stood alone among the gravestones until the bright sunlight made her head hurt.

So did Ted. The idea of a ghostly apparition violated every rational, scientific principle he believed in. If Ian found it so hard to accept...but Ian hadn't seen Rosalind. Ian reacted badly. How did Ted react? They hadn't been able to discuss it.

She rode back to the house with Reverend Holloway, feeling a bit guilty. She wasn't living up to her role as the grieving widow. A number of people were gathered at the house, waiting to pay their respects, to console her, to reminisce about Jason. Mrs. Lester had spread the dining room table with trays of finger sandwiches, cheese, crackers, fruit, and raw vegetables, but Rynna couldn't eat anything. She was beyond morning sickness, but the smell of Gouda nauseated her.

She wanted to talk to Ted. He didn't avoid her, but they had no chance for a private word. The required civility to relative strangers was so tiresome. She could plead a headache and go lie down until they left, but he would go too. He didn't live here anymore. She would have to wait them out. She assumed Ted, as Jason's cousin, officially one of the bereaved, would stay to the end—as if he would care about the etiquette of the matter. When she realized he was leaving, she followed him into the hall.

"Please don't go. We need to talk."

"Yes," he said. "But not today."

"When?"

"I'll call you," he said, evading the question, and seeing the expression on her face, he added quickly, "I promise."

"What's wrong?"

"Nothing. I just need a little time. Don't you?"

"Yes, I guess so, but I need you too."

He pretended he didn't feel that. "Well, here I am," he said. "Whatever good it may do you."

She saw no point in continuing. He would only evade the question, and any minute someone would come searching for her. "I won't keep you," she said conventionally, formally. "Thank you for coming." She leaned down to kiss him quickly, just for goodbye, but the moment developed into more than she'd intended.

"I was hoping you wouldn't do that," he said.

"Sorry," she said, although she wasn't. She touched his neat blond hair lightly and said, "Thank you for having it cut."

He gazed up at her. "It was little enough to do for you."

Rynna blinked back tears. "Can I do anything for you?"

"Yes," he said. "Don't cry."

No, she wouldn't. Not while he could see, anyway.

****

Ted did call Rynna the next morning, and she took it in the master bedroom. He asked at once, "What did you say to Ian Wyatt?" His tone was curious, not accusing.

"Nothing," she said, glad he couldn't see her guilty flush. She sank onto the bed. "Why?"

"He called me and said I should have you committed."

"Oh, my God. How did he get your number?"

"Called Information, I suppose."

"Oh dear," she said faintly. The situation wasn't funny, but...

"Should I?" Ted asked. "Have you committed?"

"Maybe you should. What did he say?"

"Said you rambled on about the house being haunted and what a monster Jason was."

"Oh, Ted, I didn't."

"What *did* you say?"

"I told him about Rosalind."

He was silenced for just a beat. "Did you? Jesus."

Rynna was oddly comforted. She had missed the unlikeliest things—his expressive voice, his almost predictable profanity. Nobody else would say the words in quite the same way. "I guess it was a mistake," she admitted. "But he was so sympathetic, and I needed to... He believed me about Jason, though. I'm sure he did. I showed him my neck, and he said Jason was like Alex."

"You certainly rattled him. He went on and on."

"I'm sorry he bothered you."

"It wasn't a problem." After a brief silence he said, "Rynna..."

"Yes?"

"Ian said you told him..."

"What?"

"Jason raped you."

19

"And you should have me committed. Marital rape isn't a concept Ian would recognize any more than Jason would."

"But...did he?"

"Yes," she said. She still remembered what it felt like to have her head deliberately banged against the headboard. It was the single thing she found hardest to forgive.

"You didn't tell me."

"How could I? I couldn't tell you anything without you swearing at me and threatening to kill him."

"I'm sorry," he said. "I wasn't much help, was I?"

She thought bleakly that he still wasn't, but she said only, "No. I'm sorry about Ian."

"It's all right."

The baby kicked, and she said, "Oh!" without meaning to. "Robert kicked me," she explained.

The difference in his tone was only relief that she had changed the subject. "What if it's a girl?"

"Theodora," she suggested.

"Absolutely not."

"Thea, then."

"Have a heart, Rynna." He knew she was teasing him. "Jason would've hated that."

She couldn't wait any longer. "Ted, I need to see you. When can we talk?"

"I don't know. I—I'll call you."

"That'll be a thrill," she said, "but the novelty of your phone calls is beginning to wear off. If you don't want to talk to me, don't." She hung up abruptly. *Damn. He did it again.* He always liked to get a rise out of her.

She slogged through the next few days grimly determined to live her own life, but she kept returning to a single obsession. If she and Ted could only talk, sit quietly and really talk the way they had so many other times…

She could go to his apartment, or she could invite him to dinner. He couldn't be eating a healthy diet on his own after years of relying on servants. She could tempt him with Mrs. Lester's cooking. Or they could meet somewhere. Didn't he say he was going to sell the Bentley and buy a more practical car now that Ellery was leaving? He could take her for a drive, or she could pick him up in Jason's Ferrari, if she could get up the nerve to drive it.

Before they were married, she and Jason had often sauntered along the river and talked about their future. She still valued those recollections when she could separate them from the later memories. She would like to do that with Ted, stroll along the river, talking…

She came to with a little shock. She could almost hear how the wheels would bump over the rough stone. The bridge was old and narrow, a romantic setting but not designed for wheelchairs. It was a symbol of what lay ahead. Ted was going back into the world where barriers, frustrations, and slights abounded. He knew what he was doing. He hadn't always lived like a recluse. He hadn't been hiding at Stonebridge, had he?

Why did she know so little about his past? Sylvia? Where did he meet her anyway? What did she know about her? Damn little. Sylvia and Ted had been "sort of engaged," and she gave him a copy of *War and Peace* for his birthday. She liked to dance, and she left. Not much to know about the only other serious relationship in his life.

When they had talked about it before, when he asked

her, hypothetically at least, to marry him, she had thought only in terms of the two of them. An entire world existed beyond Stonebridge, and living in it wouldn't always be easy. She had encountered only a little of the inherent difficulty—the discreet stares on campus and the automatic assumption he was a veteran. He met the problem with more humor than resentment, but he would inevitably be hurt sometimes. His friends and colleagues at the university respected him, but in the real world he would constantly have to deal with strangers.

What would her own life be as his wife? She understood so little of his work. Even the more elementary textbooks he edited were Greek to her. She knew nothing about the social responsibilities of a faculty wife. Was she up to a new way of life, to so many changes? Yes, something in her rose to the challenge. She was almost eager for it.

She loved Ted, who could be so difficult, who had so many defenses, beyond her own understanding. He could bruise her with his occasional bitterness, his stubbornness, his reticence, his eternal mocking irony. But those traits were balanced by so many more— intelligence, humor, courage, resilience, a newly discovered tenderness, his intense feeling for her.

Oh, Ted, I can't bear this silence between us.

****

Rynna called the number Ted had given her, but he didn't answer. Of course, he would have things to do. He wasn't sitting at home waiting for her to call.

Why would he want to marry her anyway? He cherished his privacy and independence. Wouldn't he be happier alone? He was always telling her she was a pain in the neck, and she talked too much. He wouldn't be lonely without her. Indeed, with all those skinny, free-spirited freshman girls running around, why would he want to bother with his recently widowed, pregnant cousin? The idea made her feel middle-aged. She was twenty-three.

She called again later, and he answered on the second ring, sounding absentminded, "Yeah, Demeray."

"Do you always answer the phone like that?"

"Oh, Rynna," he said. "Wait a minute." She waited. "Hi," he said. "How are you?"

"Fine. If you're busy, I can call back."

"No, it's okay. Just getting comfortable."

She wasn't comfortable—she was standing next to the bed, too restless to sit still.

"I miss you," he said.

The words brought a lump to her throat. "Why?" she asked. "Too quiet?"

"I wish. You were right about Mrs. Katz. She's caught me in the hall a couple of times, and it takes half an hour to get away. She reads the papers."

"Do you?"

"I try not to. She asks a lot of questions, but she never waits for the answers, which is just as well."

"It's too bad. It's a nice place." She didn't want to talk to him on the phone. She couldn't tell what he was thinking. Not that it was particularly easy in person. "The reason I called—"

"I knew you had an ulterior motive."

"Don't be rude. I have to go through Jason's things, his clothes and everything. Cy and Vic said they would take care of his office files and assume some of his cases, but all these personal effects… If you would help me, it wouldn't take so long. He was your cousin too." She didn't mean to sound reproachful.

"Yes, I suppose so," he said without enthusiasm. "When do you want me to come?"

"When you have time. Tomorrow? You could stay for dinner."

"I don't think so. I'll come in the morning if it's okay."

"That would be fine."

"All right. I'll see you tomorrow."

****

Ted arrived early. He probably wanted to get the job over with. Rynna waited for him in Grandmother's old room, the room she and Jason had shared, with its handsome paneling and antique four-poster. Sorting through his belongings was unappealing, even as an excuse to see Ted, but she had to do it sometime.

"Good morning," he said soberly.

She answered calmly, taking her cue from him. Cardboard boxes lay on the bed and the floor, and she was taking clothes out of the closet. The faint scent of Jason's favorite cologne made her queasy.

"Where shall I start?" Ted asked.

She held up a suit jacket. "You can have any of his things you want. I mean his clothes."

"No thanks."

"Some of them are good quality, Ted. Real silk ties."

"I don't like ties."

"Too bad. You look so handsome in a suit. I'll give them all away, then. You can start with the desk. Anything you think I should keep, leave on top. Legal papers and such in this box." She pointed. "Mr. Baxter said he would go through them. If you find any letters from old girl friends, don't tell me." She was careful to keep a businesslike tone and a reasonable distance. She sat on the bed and folded shirts into a box, and he came and put a hand on her knee to get her attention.

"Don't get fresh," she said.

"How've you been?" he asked.

"You know what they say—as well as can be expected."

"Really, are you all right?"

"Yes, Ted."

"Can you sleep?"

"Off and on. Why this sudden concern?"

"It's not sudden. No morning sickness?"

"I'm fine. Is this a house call, Doctor?"

"No, I won't charge you for it." He brushed her hair back from her face and kissed her. Not a lover's kiss, but gentle and warm.

She thanked him with a smile but chided, "Stop goofing off and get to work."

They didn't talk much at first, each busy with separate tasks. He asked her what she wanted to do with a few items and how she was managing the household accounts but had little else to say. Still, her tension eased. Something had changed. He was more himself.

Some of Grandmother's things were still in the desk, tucked away after the room was redone and forgotten. She told him he could have them, but he wasn't sentimental about objects and tossed most of them into the discard pile.

"Do you want the photograph albums?" he asked. There were only two of them, the ones he had brought upstairs for Grandmother to work on when she was bedridden.

"Oh, yes." She took them from him and caressed the

bindings with reverent fingers. "I should keep them up," she said. "I don't care about the older ones in the drawing room. You can have those."

"If you don't want them," he said. He liked the daguerreotypes, and she would set them aside for him. Grandmother had been so proud of these albums but had added little in recent years. She should save them as a visual representation of his heritage for Robert. She would like him to have the sense of family history Ted and Grandmother had shared. She opened the first album. "Now who's goofing off?" Ted chided.

"I've been at this longer than you have." She turned the pages and scanned for pictures of Ted. She found the photo of him as a child that had once sent her from the drawing room in tears. He was frowning because the sun was in his eyes. Pain might not be the only explanation for his serious expression.

"More pictures," he said, handing her a stack of fat envelopes marked *Photographs.*

Rynna put the album aside and opened one of them. It held a jumble of pictures, most of them marked with names and dates on the back. "These aren't recent," she told him.

"She didn't put everything in the albums." Not, for instance, any pictures of Rosalind after she met Alexander Wyatt.

Rynna didn't need a label to recognize Clara, slender and smiling, wearing an awful hat and holding an infant in her arms. "Your mother," she said, and he took the picture and studied it. Something of Clara was in his face, not features, but fleeting expressions, like the softened look on his face now. He handed the photo back, and she turned it over to check the date. Ted wasn't the baby Clara held, according to the handwriting on the back. It was William Jr.

She glanced through the pictures quickly and laid most of them aside but lingered over several interesting ones. The logic of Grandmother's selections for the albums escaped her. Why, for instance, didn't she choose this attractive shot of Ted in graduation cap and gown?

He handed her another packet. "Your wedding pictures."

She should have put these in an album too, but she found herself completely indifferent to them. She would select a few to keep for Robert. She set them aside and continued to sort the Demeray family photos.

She found another good shot of Ted—at first, she noticed only him, sitting in the wheelchair in front of a desk or table, smiling confidently into the camera. He appeared incredibly young, but the picture couldn't have been taken many years ago. Seated on the table with one hand on his shoulder was a long-legged blonde in a blue sundress, tanned, healthy, laughing. "Who is this?" she asked, and even before she handed it to him, she knew. A good-looking girl, Sylvia, but what sort of woman could put such light in his eyes and then extinguish it?

He took the picture but didn't answer her question. He glanced at it and handed it back. His expression didn't suggest that he was grieving for a lost love.

"She was beautiful, wasn't she?" Rynna asked. Was that the right tense? Sylvia was presumably still alive.

"Are you fishing? She didn't have your kind of beauty, but she was very pretty."

Yes, a pretty girl, fun-loving, vibrant, good-natured. She liked to dance. He had never looked like that with Rynna, but nothing had ever been easy or carefree between them. "She broke your heart," she said.

"More likely she hurt my pride," he said. "Why do you want to talk about Sylvia?"

She shrugged and returned to the pictures. She hesitated over a photo of William and Clara for so long that Ted came to see what she was doing. Studying his father, who was sturdy, blond, and intelligent looking, she said, "Once when I was talking to Grandmother, she called you William by mistake."

"Yes, she did sometimes."

"You are like him. Are you sure you're adopted?"

He laughed and took the picture out of her hands. "Yes."

"I saw the stone for William Jr. after the funeral," she told him. "Ian said it was the saddest thing of all, to bury a child. He was so sympathetic. Ian, I mean. Until I mentioned Rosalind."

He set the photo aside and met her gaze. Rynna let the pictures she held drop to the floor unheeded. Finally, haltingly, they talked about the night Jason died. Whatever euphoria he had experienced after living through the ordeal had dimmed, and they shared a certain guilt in their survival.

"You weren't even scared," she said.

"Yes, I was. There is something particularly nasty about a handgun."

"I know you were in a lot of pain," she ventured. "Ellery said—"

"He said I looked as if I had seen a ghost." Irony, his favorite refuge.

"You don't believe in ghosts."

"No." He was silent for a long time before he said, "The fact is Jason damn near killed us both. Rosalind was all that saved us, and maybe it isn't up to us to question how it was done."

"But it's awful to think of Rosalind—her own son."

"I wish I could have—if I could have grabbed the gun…"

"I knew you would think that. I was afraid you would try. You couldn't have done anything you didn't, Ted. Nothing."

"If I hadn't let go, he would've passed out in another minute."

"Or you would've killed him and gone to prison."

"No…"

"I was so afraid…"

Talking about it wasn't easy, but having it out in the open was a relief.

Presently they had no more words to say, and they worked diligently with only an occasional remark about Jason's belongings. Once Rynna put the pictures aside, the task was quickly done.

Rynna asked Ted to stay for lunch. "Pot roast," she said with a smile. In all the months she had known him, he had never expressed a preference about food. He ate whatever was in front of him. She didn't have much hope of tempting him with home cooking.

"No, thank you," he said politely and kissed her goodbye. When Grandmother died, he had been bitter about Rynna inheriting Stonebridge. Now he seemed indifferent, but surely he couldn't have grown up in so magnificent a house and not harbor some sentiment for it. Maybe it wasn't the house he was indifferent to now.

Later in the afternoon, Rynna had another shock. Baxter, the family lawyer, called on her to discuss the will. Jason had left a great deal of money, nothing like the fortune Ted inherited from Grandmother, but enough to keep her comfortably for some time. Knowing Jason, she might have anticipated the catch, a provision in the will that if she remarried within two years of his death, everything would go to Ian and Janet.

She could give Robert Jason's money, or she could give him Ted's name. Ted wouldn't spend Grandmother's money on himself, nor presumably on her or Robert. He had a strange prejudice against unearned income. She might be better off financially if she didn't marry him.

Assuming the choice was hers to make, why should she marry a man who wouldn't talk about his feelings? Who, as accommodating as he had been about this baby, didn't want children, didn't want her to have his children? She didn't have to choose, did she? She wouldn't tell him about the will. The next move was his. If he didn't make it, the hell with him. She was sick to death of feeling this way—bruised, humiliated, in limbo.

Chapter Three

Ted made the next move. He wrote Rynna a letter.

Lucy delivered the mail to her as usual, without comment. She sorted through bills and circulars and condolence cards from people she didn't know before she discovered a letter addressed in an unfamiliar hand to Rynna Dalton Wyatt. No return address. He had typewritten the letter, which was like him.

Dear Cousin, he began. What was that? An endearment? An affectionate nickname? An ironic one? A reminder that she had only recently considered any relationship between them incestuous?

Dear Cousin,

I'm not much of a letter writer, as you'll see, but if I call you on the phone you'll hang up if you don't like what I have to say. If I see you, I'll kiss you and lose my train of thought. I've thought a lot about this, and I hope you'll understand what I'm going to say. Less than a year ago, I saw you married to Jason. You went to him willingly, happily. Anyone could see that. The fact that Jason betrayed your trust doesn't change anything. He was a bastard, but you loved him. Having had that once, even though it didn't last, you could never settle for second best.

The other day I asked you if you would consider marrying me, and you said yes. I had no right to ask. I have no right to ask anything of you. Remember that this has all taken place in a matter of days, during a time when you were confused and under stress. You are too intelligent to make any decision on such a basis. I know a lot of what you think you feel for me started with seeing me as a way out. If you needed that and I gave it to you, I'm glad I was able to.

Now you are free. You have a lot of options, and you have to make an intelligent choice. I think you are stronger than you realize. You don't need to lean on anyone. You may not believe it right now, but you will. When you are ready to make decisions about your future, I don't want you to imagine you have any obligation to me. You don't. I am proud to have been your friend and your cousin. Nothing that has happened recently should be allowed to change that.

I hope you can make sense of this. I did warn you I was no letter writer.

Ted

Rynna was not deceived. This curious missive was a love letter.

It might be true that she'd seen him as a way out. It might also be true that he took advantage of her. Not in any of the usual ways, but to free her from Jason. Now, as he said, she was free. All right, maybe he didn't want to marry her, but his feelings were more than cousinly. She had known that since her wedding day when he kissed her goodbye so intimately.

I don't want you to imagine you have any obligation to me. Was he so unsure of her? Or was this a way to evade his own obligation? She couldn't blame him for regretting a hypothetical question that was now unexpectedly a possibility.

But he did want her physically. She couldn't be

wrong about the attraction between them. He certainly liked kissing her, and they were friends first, which was the best way.

If I see you, I'll kiss you and lose my train of thought.
Yes, it was a love letter.

****

Rynna didn't even call to make sure Ted was home. She took the chance that he would be out for hours or would have company. She didn't want him to have time to think about this meeting and marshal his arguments. She drove the Ferrari, a daring adventure with both the foreign gearshift and the unfamiliar roads to contend with. If she could drive Jason's car, she could work out her own future.

She parked around the corner, so Ted wouldn't come back and spot the Ferrari and know she was waiting for him. She counted on the element of surprise to tell her what she needed to know. She braced herself for an encounter with Mrs. Katz, the building manager, and hurried through the lobby—*Demeray* was neatly lettered on one of the mailboxes—to the elevator.

He had only lived here for a few days, but this was his home ground, as his room at Stonebridge had been. Why was she always going to him? As he said, he'd never had any right to come to her. She had been Jason's wife. Now she wasn't.

She rang the doorbell. Less than a minute passed until he opened the door, ready with an expression of polite inquiry. "Rynna!" Was he pleased? A little, but he had a guilty flush, as if he were embarrassed about the letter.

"Hello, Ted." She glanced around the small, attractively furnished living room to give him a few seconds to collect himself. Boxes of books were everywhere, most of them unopened. He hadn't done much unpacking.

"I'm sorry about the mess. Please sit down. The sofa isn't bad."

She sat on the sofa. Among more books on the coffee table was an ashtray with two half-smoked cigarettes snubbed out in it. She immediately averted her gaze so he wouldn't notice she had seen them.

"Can I get you something?" he asked. "Coffee or tea or…?"

"Do you have anything cold?" she asked. The weather was hot and muggy today, with an oppressive overcast that threatened thunder.

"Only beer, I'm afraid, and milk."

"Coffee, then, if it's no trouble." She should drink milk, for Robert's sake, but it didn't appeal.

"No trouble," he said. She studied the titles of the books on the coffee table while he was in the kitchen. He didn't take long. He cleared a space to set the cup, moving a few books and the ashtray. "Oh," he said, as if he owed her an explanation. "Don Casper and Fred Sullivan were here. We played basketball, and they came up for a beer."

"Basketball," she said doubtfully, and took a sip of coffee—instant, but not bad.

"Wheelchair basketball. We used to play all the time." He smiled, half amused, half daring. "Did you think I'd had a woman up here?"

"That's your business," she said. "I have no claim on you."

He looked away. "No, I suppose not."

"Is that what you've been doing? Playing

basketball?"

He shrugged. "Getting settled in, shopping for a car, a department meeting, class prep…"

"Writing letters," she added.

"I'm sorry," he said. "It was easier."

"No doubt. But I think we should talk."

"Would you like to go out somewhere? There's an Italian place—"

"No, I don't think so."

"I don't have much in the refrigerator, but we could have something delivered."

"You don't have to feed me, Ted. I just want to talk." She didn't like to refuse his hospitality, but she wasn't hungry. "You could show me the rest of the apartment," she suggested.

"It's a mess," he warned her, and of course she'd seen it before, but he led the way, no doubt welcoming the distraction. Books were piled everywhere, even in the kitchen. They were almost the only signs of habitation. His clothes hung in the half-open closet in the bedroom, and a green chenille spread adorned the bed.

"This is new," she said, indicating the polished oak desk, bigger but no more pretentious than the one in his room at Stonebridge.

"Yes," he said. "The rest you've seen."

She stood at the window and gazed out at the view. The air had darkened even in the few minutes she had been here. "Is it going to rain?" she asked.

"Probably."

Rynna took a deep breath and turned away from the window. "Do you remember the last time I was here, in this room?"

"I won't hold you to anything you said while Jason

was alive," he said.

"Coward."

"Yes, all right. I don't want you to make a mistake."

"Another mistake, you mean." She moved on to the desk, fingered the uncovered typewriter, and studied the titles of the books. On the other side of the typewriter, where she almost missed it, was a small, framed photograph of her, one Grandmother had commissioned when her hair was shorter. "Where did you get this?" she asked.

Caught, he confessed. "I stole it."

"Ted…" She was terribly touched. She had been belligerent, combative. If he didn't want to marry her, he would have to say so. Now she only wanted to be in his arms again, to tell him how much she loved him. She sat in the chair and met his gaze, and he took pity on her and came to take her hands in his. "What are we going to do?" she asked.

"Whatever you say. I meant what I wrote in the letter. You need time to make an intelligent decision."

She shook her head. "You're just scared. I know you, Ted."

"Do you?" His gaze, avoiding hers, was on their linked hands. She loved his hands—strong and well-shaped, the sleeves of his shirt rolled up, wiry blond hair on his wrists.

"It's all right," she said. "Everybody is."

Then he did look at her. "You weren't when you married Jason."

"Yes, of course I was, but I'd made up my mind, and I sure as hell wasn't going to tell you about my doubts."

"If you had, I might have stopped you."

"You tried. You couldn't." She had been so

determined, so positive, so wrong. "Maybe you're right," she said. "We should wait. Not see each other for a while and think things through. The whole thing with Jason is too recent. I need time to put it behind me."

He was relieved and couldn't hide it. "How long?" he asked.

"I don't know." If she had divorced Jason, they would have had to wait a year. Social convention would dictate doing so after his death as well. "Maybe until after the baby is born. Six months or so."

"That's too long," he said at once.

"Ted!"

"I'm sorry," he said, laughing at himself. "It's just— when you said that, it sounded so long. Six months…"

They weren't getting anywhere. She would take a while to get over Jason, and he would have to put up with that whether they were together or apart. He said it was her decision. Fine. She hadn't come here to seduce him, but it might be better to take the edge off curiosity and desire and make a clear-headed decision.

"Ted, I want you to make love to me."

He stared at her, his hands on hers, and didn't answer.

"Don't you want to?"

He didn't answer, but she could tell he did. Desperately. After a moment he said, "I know you think I'm…"

"Old-fashioned?" She did, yes. "What I think," she told him gently, "is that you made one mistake, and it hurt enough that you're still gun-shy."

He didn't admit anything, but he asked, "How did you get to be so smart?"

"Maybe I learned from my mistakes. Sometimes

you have to take risks."

He kissed her, and all the dizzying emotion that had frightened her so much when Jason might have found out gripped her again. "Are you sure?" he whispered, with his hands in her hair.

"Yes," she said. She wasn't, but he needed her to be.

He let go of her and switched on the small portable radio on the bedside table. Light background music at low volume. "Turn off the light," he said. She was nearer the switch.

"Why?" she asked. Jason never had. "I've seen your legs," she reminded him.

He gave her a longsuffering look and did it himself. The room wasn't completely dark but romantically dim, with the music as background. She sat on the bed and waited for him to come to her. "Are you always this much trouble?" he asked and kissed her.

"Sorry," she murmured. She hoped they wouldn't regret this. Sitting together on the bed, kissing, was lovely, but she didn't know how seriously Ted might take it. She had meant to make the decision clearer, but he might believe they had made a commitment. She didn't want him to be obligated to marry her.

She was shy and a little awkward with him now. They knew each other too well for casual sex but not deeply enough for easy intimacy. If he kept kissing her, though, she would forget everything.

He couldn't manage the buttons on her blouse, and she had to help him, and they both laughed, which helped a lot. Dizzy, breathless, Rynna lay back against the pillows and would have pulled him down on top of her, but he stopped her. "No, Rynna," he said. "I can't."

For one furious second she thought, Don't you dare

tell me that now, and then she realized what he meant. "Oh, I'm sorry. What should I…?"

"Shut up," he said, and she relaxed against the pillows, giving up control. She had been enough trouble. Now she would let him take the lead.

Ted was trembling, his breathing uneven, as overwhelmed as she was, but he took his time, kissing and caressing her. This was what lovemaking meant. With Jason, for all his practiced skill, what she had experienced was only sex. He was never going to believe it, but Ted was first after all.

****

The oppressive heat finally broke. Thunder rumbled in the distance, and light rain spattered against the window. The air had a dusty, electric quality. Rynna lay quietly in the increasing darkness and considered her still uncertain future. Whatever happened now, she would always have this. Ted was right about one thing. She could never again settle for second best.

She turned her head a little and studied his face. His eyes were closed, but she wasn't sure he was asleep. She hoped the slight tension in his jaw muscles wasn't caused by pain, and a light sheen of sweet was only the aftermath of passion and summer heat. His face was so familiar, and yet it was strange now, mysterious. She was happier than she deserved to be, just looking at him.

He wasn't asleep. He felt her stir, opened his eyes, caressed her face, and then rested his hand on her abdomen.

"I wish I could be slim and beautiful for you," she whispered.

"You *are* beautiful," he said. "All pregnant women are."

"Is that why you love me?"

"I don't know why I love you."

She was silent. She felt loved now, lying with him like this, but this was unreal, wasn't it? The darkness and the radio still playing softly, the eerie weather. She had been happy like this with Jason at first, before she lost him to his jealous delusions, his certainty that if she slept with him, she must sleep with other men as well, and now she had all but seduced Ted. "Do you think I'm a whore?" she asked.

"A—Jesus, Rynna! Is that how I made you feel?"

"Oh, no, Ted. You made me feel loved. I'm sorry. Jason—"

"Jason was full of shit."

"I wish I could forget he ever existed, but I can't. I wish—"

"Don't wish. It doesn't help." He kissed her. "I'm sorry I snapped at you."

"You didn't." She stroked his face. Talking to him like this was so easy, as if usual restraints didn't apply. She could say anything, ask anything—a dangerous assumption. "I'm sure it's wrong to be this happy," she said. "Nothing has been solved."

"No," he agreed. "Except now you know."

"Now I know. I should get up and make something to eat. If I could borrow a robe, I'd scramble some eggs or something."

"You can borrow anything you want, but you don't have to cook for me. You're not my wife, much less my servant, and this is my apartment. If you're hungry—"

"No." She didn't want him to do anything. He had done enough. She was hungry, but she was too lazy to move. If she left this haven, she might never find it again.

"Does Lucy know where you are?' he asked. "If you're going to stay, you should call, or she'll worry."

"Do you want me to stay?"

"I don't know," he said truthfully, and she was happier with that than she would've been with an easy lie.

"Ted," she ventured. "Does it hurt...?"

"Oh, Rynna," he said, irritated.

"I know, but if I don't ask, I'll just worry about it."

"Well, don't."

"But does it?"

"It hurts to get out of bed in the morning," he said. "If I let it stop me, I might as well be dead."

"Ted..."

"More questions?" he asked, but he wasn't displeased. She talked too much, but he loved her anyway.

"You know how to shut me up," she said, so he kissed her, and she nestled quietly in his arms for several minutes.

This time she was on dangerous ground, but she couldn't help herself. This intimacy was like truth serum. She braced for his reaction. "Did you sleep with Sylvia?"

Silence. None of her business. "Yes," he said. His voice had an unfamiliar tone. She was sorry she'd asked.

As if he could read her mind, Ted said, "I told you you could ask me anything."

What he had said was he wouldn't smack her for asking. She almost wished he would. She was used to being hurt. "I know it isn't any of my business," she apologized. Sylvia couldn't have been this much trouble. She was probably perfect. "Ted..."

"Shut up," he said. "I love you."

Chapter Four

Ted and Rynna were married two weeks later.

It was too soon, of course. Jason hadn't been dead a month. It was, by any accepted standard, indecent haste. But to wait any longer was, as Ted had said, to wait too long. Rynna was nearly six months pregnant, and she wanted her child to be born with the Demeray name. Two weeks wasn't long to prepare to begin a new life together. Ted was busy preparing for the classes he would be teaching, and now they had additional details to take care of. The campus apartment wouldn't be big enough for long, and finding a suitable house was a top priority. If their marriage created a scandal in the university community, life under Mrs. Katz's roof would become unbearable.

The problem of Stonebridge had weighed on Rynna's mind for some time. She didn't want to live in the house any longer, and Ted's life was elsewhere now. But to allow it to go out of the family, when Grandmother had so much wanted the line to continue there, would be disloyal and ungrateful.

Ted wasn't at all concerned when she broached the subject over a take-out lunch at his apartment. "We'll lease it," he said at once. Baxter would take care of the arrangements, he assured her. The money it earned, like the trust fund Grandmother had left her, was hers, as the house was hers. Ted wouldn't touch it. She must never be any more dependent on him than she chose to be.

She told him Jason had left everything to Ian Wyatt, in trust for his children. He studied her gravely and said, "I'd rather you didn't lie to me, Rynna."

"Baxter told you?" she asked in a small voice. "I didn't want you to think I was giving up anything to marry you."

"Money is the least of what you're giving up," he said.

Yes, that might be true, but she wouldn't be giving up anything of consequence and certainly not as much as he would. He was about to begin a new life. He didn't need to take on any additional burdens. "Did you think if we went to bed together that one time you would have to marry me?" she asked.

"No. I thought you would decide to go back to Colorado."

Rynna was amazed. Colorado was a lifetime ago. Would he ever be sure of her?

At every step of their plans, he deferred to her, not out of indecision, but in recognition of how much he was asking of her. He'd made up his mind what kind of life he was going to live, and he wanted her to share it. Whatever he could do to make it easier, he would do.

The wedding preparations were even more unreal than Jason's funeral. What did this mean, these decisions, this piece of paper? During the flurry of preparations for her first wedding, the license was a minor detail. This time she studied it intently. The document declared that Rynna Dalton Wyatt, widow, and Theodore Scott Demeray, bachelor, intended to commit matrimony. A rash undertaking, surely. It also said they were "no relation" to each other. Rynna was afraid someone might challenge this, but Baxter said no. While they were legally first cousins, for purposes of marriage they were "no relation," although she felt more related to him than ever.

She wore a navy-blue suit with a plain white silk blouse, no frills. Ted surprised her with a corsage delivered to Stonebridge on the morning of the wedding, pale pink and white, lovely against the dark blue, and suitable for a bride still theoretically in mourning. She pinned the sweet-scented flowers to her jacket in front of the mirror, and her spirits lifted. She wasn't the storybook bride who'd marched down the aisle to marry Jason, but she was a woman in love.

She removed the old-fashioned wedding band Jason had given her, the ring that had been Rosalind's. Ted wouldn't have minded if she kept it, but she didn't want to go to him with anything more of Jason than she could help. She took the ring to the music room and laid it on top of Rosalind's piano. She waited, listening, but she sensed nothing, no slightest vibration. Rosalind was at rest now.

Ted picked her up in his new car. The interior was tasteful and bore a distinctive new-car smell. She was nervous, not about the wedding, but about his driving. Jason had always driven so fast, sometimes recklessly, and she was used to Ellery chauffeuring them in the Bentley and didn't expect Ted to be a good driver.

He was. He knew the roads a lot better than she did, and he stayed under the speed limit. She relaxed, and as he took the first bend beside the river, she smiled at him. "Handles nicely," he said, taking the compliment for the car instead of himself. She hoped he would find his new wife as manageable.

They didn't talk much on the drive. The mileage he hoped to get, the weather—sunny, not as cool as they had hoped, but not bad. It was September, after all. She thanked him for the corsage, and he said she looked great. He did too, but she didn't say so. He wore his one dark suit, but the shirt might be new. His hair, cut a few weeks ago for Jason's funeral, now brushed his collar in back. Funny how it touched her, the straight blond hair on the back of his neck, his hands resting on the steering wheel. She wanted very much to kiss him.

After he parked the car, she did so. He smoothed her hair but didn't kiss her back. He was nervous now, a little. "We're early," he said. Only a few cars were parked in the church lot, but traffic flowed past on the street. The sun, beating straight down, made waiting in the car too warm.

They went inside, where it was cool and dim. Rynna hadn't wanted to ask Reverend Holloway to marry them, since he'd so recently married her to Jason, and the Brenford church had all those awful stone steps. This new, modern church, convenient to the university, was the logical choice. Reverend Smith—a wonderfully anonymous name—was courteous and accommodating. He had discreetly avoided staring at her waistline, but he must think they had to get married. She didn't mind if Ted didn't.

They were to be married in the study, not the echoing church. Simple, quiet, no fuss. She'd had her dream wedding, and where had it brought her? Pregnant, widowed, confused, and exactly where she wanted to be today, come to Reverend Smith's study to be married to this man. His secretary ushered them inside and left them alone. A big old-fashioned clock ticked loudly in the silent room, impeccably decorated with dark wood, a lace-curtained window, and plush carpet.

Ted cleared his throat. "Are you sure you want to go through with this?" he asked.

"I am. Are you having second thoughts?"

"Not for me. For you. I'm no bargain."

"I don't want a bargain." She studied him, tried to read his thoughts. He was so damned serious. This was his first marriage and not something he would take lightly. "You are very special to me," she said. "Don't you know that?"

He shook his head. "If you say so." He kissed her and then gave her a rare, genuine smile, worth waiting for.

The secretary returned with Reverend Smith, jovial and kind, ready to put them at ease. Ted's hand closed on Rynna's. The secretary perched on a straight chair, ready to do her duty as witness. Seated comfortably in an armchair in her flat shoes and matronly dark blue suit, but with Ted's corsage pinned to her jacket and her hair down her back, Rynna couldn't have felt more like a bride.

"Theodore Scott Demeray, will you take this woman, Rynna Dalton Wyatt, as your lawful wedded wife...?"

"Yes, I will."

Those words, so familiar, so nearly the same as with Jason. What was Ted thinking? He was very serious, his gaze intent on her while he waited for her to make her response.

"I will."

He held the plain gold band he had insisted on buying and repeated, "Receive this ring as a token of love and fidelity." It slipped easily onto her finger, his hand cool and steady on hers, and she was married to him, only weeks after swearing that, if she could ever be free of Jason, she would never marry again. And despite that, no regret, no fear, no stab of panic. The commitment was simple. She only needed to gaze into Ted's eyes.

He kissed her, and she detected something new in his manner, a kind of shy sweetness she liked, and quiet, unpossessive pride.

No guests, no flowers, no music, all accomplished quickly and efficiently. The ceremony was a simple one, a solemn contract between two people, and anything else was an unnecessary frill.

Reverend Smith kissed her cheek and called her "Mrs. Demeray" for the first time. Amid the flurry of thanks, congratulations, and farewells, Ted said almost nothing.

In the car, he recovered his casual tone and asked if she wanted to go to a restaurant.

"No," she said. "The hotel."

They had reserved a room for two nights, not so much in the spirit of a honeymoon as to avoid Mrs. Katz. Rynna took off her corsage and put it away in its box. She wore—and needed—maternity clothes, and people on the street tended to stare at her as much as at Ted in his wheelchair. Now she knew what it was like, except people smiled when they saw her. Nevertheless, she didn't want the hotel clerk to think they were newlyweds.

She did feel like a bride, certainly more than she felt like a mother. This would be her wedding night, and she looked forward to it with something more than anticipation. They hadn't made love after the first time. As important as that was, it had also been difficult—a little awkward, a little desperate. Neither of them had been sure this was the right thing to do. Now the decision had been made, and they were married.

Married. Mrs. Demeray. She looked at Ted. He kept his gaze on the road and said, "You're very quiet. Are you sorry already?"

"No, I was afraid you might be. I can just hear you thinking, My God, this woman is going to drive me crazy for the rest of my life."

"No doubt you will."

"I'll try not to." She touched the hair at the back of his neck. She couldn't resist any longer. "Did I tell you I love you?" She rested her hand on his knee.

"Rynna, I'm driving."

"Drive a little faster," she said.

****

The hotel clerk at the Brenford Inn was indifferent to anything except their reservation. Ted signed the register in his clear, straightforward handwriting, *Mr. and Mrs. T. S. Demeray.* She didn't see what he gave the bellhop, but the young man grinned and said, "Thank you, sir."

When the door was closed, she said, "I thought you were trying to live within your income."

"The publisher's paying for this," Ted told her. "So if you want caviar or lobster, this is your opportunity." She hadn't seen the check from the publisher, but the amount was apparently substantial.

"I'm not hungry," she said. Their eyes met.

"I'll order champagne," he said. "You can't have a wedding without champagne."

"You keep telling me I shouldn't drink."

"You shouldn't. But a glass of champagne on your

wedding day won't hurt at this stage."

While he called room service, she took off her jacket and hung it in the closet. The room was welcoming, not luxurious enough to make her feel out of place, but comfortable. The bed was big and soft, with a cheerful yellow spread. Afternoon sunlight slanted through the single window.

She loosened Ted's tie. "Thank you," he said. "That's much better." He pulled her down, so she sat on the armrest of the wheelchair. She wasn't sure it was safe, but she put her arm around him, and they kissed for a long, blissful moment.

"Could I sit on your lap?" she asked.

"Carefully."

She decided not to risk it and undid the top button of his shirt.

"Wait," he said.

She waited.

A middle-aged waiter delivered the champagne. He gave them a smile. He knew an occasion for champagne when he saw one. Ted tipped him, and he said, "Thank you, sir!" in the same tone the bellhop had used.

Rynna sat on the bed, and Ted poured the champagne. "To the three of us," he said and raised his glass. It wasn't a traditional wedding toast, but it would serve. The taste was exactly sweet enough, and the bubbles tickled her nose.

When she had sipped enough champagne—a limit she reached quickly—Rynna kissed Ted and said, "I'll just be a minute." While she was in the bathroom, she began to feel strange. Was the champagne affecting her? She had no reason to be nervous. He loves me, she thought. She was safe. Maybe the setting was the problem—something a little unsettling about hotel rooms? No matter. She would be all right in a minute.

No, the room in the Bahamas was nothing like this, not at all. Jason had deliberately banged her head on the headboard a second time after she had fallen against it. *No. No.*

In a moment she was calm again. The bad moment was nothing, the kind of involuntary memory people suffered when they had been through a war. Jason was dead. Ted was waiting.

Once they were sitting together on the edge of the bed, kissing, she had no misgivings. Her hair swung forward across her face, and he brushed it back, his hand warm and gentle on her cheek. She was overcome by the familiar, dizzying sense of falling toward him, into him, and his arms were around her, strong and steadying, to keep her safe. "I love you," she said.

He undid the top two buttons of her blouse, which gave her a pleasurable little thrill, but when he touched her throat, not at all roughly, she winced, gasped, and backed away. Just for a second...

"God, I'm sorry," he said at once. "Did I...?" He was bewildered.

"No, no," she said desperately, half in tears. "You didn't hurt me." His face was etched with real concern. He didn't know Jason had never touched her that way, had never put his hand on her throat except with violent intent, to choke or restrain her. "God damn Jason," she cried. "How dare he do this to me?"

"Jason," he said, resigned. He didn't try to put his arms around her again but sat where he was and waited. Rynna had betrayed him and let Jason come between them.

"Why did I *let* him? I should have left him the first time he hit me. I should have known." She wept bitterly.

Ted let her cry and didn't touch her. When she finally stopped crying, he poured a little champagne into her glass and made her drink it before he took her in his arms as if she were a child and comforted her, patient and resigned.

"I'm sorry," she said.

"It's all right," he assured her. "I expect it was overdue. I think you should have something to eat now, and then maybe you can get some sleep."

"No, Ted. I wanted to—"

"We have lots of time," he said. Lots of time—did they? They had already been through so much waiting. She didn't even know how long he'd waited for her without saying anything when she was foolish enough to think she was in love with Jason. *Damn Jason.*

Theorizing that a change of scene couldn't hurt, they ate dinner at a restaurant, a handsomely appointed eatery with an attentive staff and prompt service. The food was good too, and Rynna ate more than she expected—tender filet mignon, perfectly browned potatoes, and a crisp green salad. When they returned, the hotel room was familiar enough to make her a little more at home.

She did fall asleep, finally, on the big, soft, comfortable bed, with Ted lying fully clothed next to her. He stayed on his side of the bed and didn't touch her. Had he stopped wanting her? Did he believe she still belonged to Jason?

In the morning she felt much better. Things appeared less daunting in sunlight, as they always did. The events of yesterday were unreal, absurd. All except the part where Ted put the ring on her finger and kissed her so sweetly.

"Hey," she said, nudging him awake.

"Good morning," he said.

"You look very uncomfortable," she told him, "sleeping in your clothes." She kissed him and rubbed her hand over his cheek. He had a light stubble, blonder than his hair. "I'm sorry about last night. Do you feel deprived?"

"No, just very lucky." He kissed her.

"Which isn't such a compliment," she reminded him. "You said the same thing about having arthritis."

"Well," he said, "of the two..."

Rynna laughed. It was good to laugh again.

She called room service while Ted shaved and showered. They savored scrambled eggs, orange juice, rich, hot coffee, and flaky croissants with sweet butter and marmalade. She remembered tea and biscuits and jam at Stonebridge, now so far away, and asked, "Do you know how many times we've eaten breakfast together?"

"Hundreds," he said, "but none as nice as this."

"You are sweet when you want to be," she told him.

"Thank you," he said, trying not to show his embarrassment.

"Ted." She put down her coffee cup and reached for his hand. "I love you." She couldn't wait any longer.

In spite of herself, she was at first only half willing, but Ted was patient, content to kiss her and stroke her hair until she was ready. He wasn't like Jason in any way. He undressed her slowly, as if prolonging the pleasure of opening a special gift. Nothing in their lovemaking could remind her of Jason's need to dominate and possess her. Her fear of hurting him vanished quickly too. She was exhilarated to discover she need think of nothing at all except loving Ted and being loved. Having the hotel room for a second night would be a good thing. Without room service, they would go hungry.

"Was it like this with Sylvia?" she asked him, lying with her head on his shoulder, her hair spilling across his chest.

"Rynna!"

"I know, shut up, but you said—"

"One of these days I might smack you anyway. I understand why Jason is still between us, but Sylvia is history."

"She wasn't when we first met." He didn't answer, and she shifted so she could see his face, with its familiar stubborn expression. "I'm sorry," she said. "I know I should mind my own business, but this is so nice, lying here with you, talking. Don't you think it's nice?"

"Much too nice. I start work tomorrow. You've shot my concentration all to hell."

"No, you'll be great. Tell me what you're going to teach them."

"Geochemistry," he said with a smile. "It would put you to sleep."

"Why would it? *You* like it. Could I take your class?"

He considered this. "Did you take geology in college?"

"No." Her general education courses had included only one science class. "I got a B in chemistry."

"You could take mineralogy. It's not as interesting, but the only prerequisite is chemistry. It's too late to register for credit, but—"

"Ted, do you mean you would let me?"

"Let you? I don't know how I would stop you."

"But wouldn't you mind? If it was me, if I was going to teach a class, I wouldn't want you in the room."

"You're prettier than I am," he said.

Rynna nestled closer. "Every time I think I know you, you surprise me again."

Chapter Five

The following morning Ted and Rynna checked out of the Brenford Inn, not without regret, and returned to the apartment building. Nobody was in the lobby when they entered, and Ted told Rynna to go on upstairs while he checked the mail. As the elevator doors closed, a door opened, and Mrs. Katz's blunt voice called, "Mr. Demeray!"

Fifteen minutes passed before he came up to the apartment, and he was seething. "We have to get out of this place," he said.

"You used to think she was funny."

"She used to be funny," he said. "Not anymore."

"Poor Ted."

"Don't, Rynna," he said. "I am not in the mood. I told her I had a class this morning. If I'm late…"

"You won't be late." She couldn't understand his bad temper. He had been angry so many times, but always about Jason. Recently, since Jason's death, she hadn't seen him like this. He was so patient, so even. Except when she had asked if he thought she was a whore. "Did she say something?"

"What do you think she was doing for the last ten minutes? God damn the woman. Where are my notes?" He rummaged in the desk and slammed drawers.

"Ted, please calm down."

He stopped searching. "I'm sorry."

She approached the desk and put her arms around him from behind.

"I'm sorry," he repeated. "I'm just edgy."

"Yes, I noticed."

He leaned his head back against her and put his hand on her arm.

"Did she say something to upset you?"

"No. I told you I wouldn't be easy to live with."

"You've been harder. Shall I help you find your notes?"

"No," he said, a bit sheepish. "They're right here."

"Could I have a kiss, then?" She shoved papers out of the way and perched on the edge of the desk.

"I expect you could." They kissed for a long moment, and then Ted put his hand on her knee.

"Fresh," she said, smiling. "We don't have time now. Anything else I can do for you, sir? A cup of coffee, maybe? Can I get you a pill?"

"I can get my own pills when I need them, thank you, and my own coffee. That's not your job."

"What is my job?"

"Love, honor…forgive."

Rynna touched his face. "Yes, all right. I'm sorry about 'Poor Ted.' I know that's one thing I should never say to you."

"One other thing you should never say to me…"

"Let me guess. 'I don't love you anymore.'?"

"No, you'd better tell me that," he said, and he almost sounded serious. "I would hate to be the last to know."

"What, then?" She waited.

Ted shifted his hand from her knee to her abdomen. He was gentle and loving. "You should never say, 'He's not your child.' I would never deny Jason was his biological father, but when you married me, he became our child. You can't raise him alone."

"No, I wouldn't want to. I promise I'll never say that." He had surprised her again, and she had a clue to what Mrs. Katz said to upset him.

****

Rynna was dismayed to discover how much work was involved in studying geology. Ted taught only two classes, but they involved thirteen hours of class time every week—four lectures and nine hours of laboratory work. A teaching assistant was assigned to grade papers, but he would handle the labs himself. Fred Sullivan approved her late registration, and she enrolled in the mineralogy course, which meant six hours of lab work. "I'm not sure I love you enough," she joked.

They entered the classroom together, Rynna conscious of privileges his other students didn't have. Professors sometimes married their students, but they had done things backward. She wandered around the room, taking in the desks and the blackboard and the old venetian blinds. She had never been there before, but the setting was familiar. Even the smell evoked her school days—chalk, cheap cleanser, and old books. "I thought I was finished with all this," she said.

Ted ignored her. He wrote on the blackboard in bold printing, plain and legible, like his handwriting. When he was finished, he left the wheelchair and sat on the desk, facing the empty classroom. He didn't project an academic image—too young, too casual, dressed more like a student in his favorite pullover sweater. Still, she'd had teachers like him and sometimes harbored crushes on them. He glanced at his notes and then laid them aside

57

and finally looked across the room at her.

"You're very quiet," she remarked. "Are you scared?"

"No," he said and added with a faint smile, "Not about this."

Footsteps approached outside the open door. Rynna sat and opened the textbook, the one she had first seen in his room at Stonebridge, so long ago, *Introduction to Mineralogy* by Christopher Powell and Theodore Demeray. She didn't want the other students to know she was his wife. They came in chatting breezily, quieted a little when they realized the professor was in the room, but kept talking as they took their seats. They were all so young—it was a lower division course—and careless, as if they hadn't yet learned anything about life. Had she been so innocent herself, only a few years ago?

The clock above the blackboard clicked loudly to mark the hour, and Ted asked a student in the front row to close the door. As if it were a signal, they all fell silent, pens poised over notebooks, alert and expectant.

"Good morning," Ted said. "This is Geology 21, and I'm Ted Demeray." He sounded like a teacher. He had become a teacher.

For fifty minutes she took notes and tried to concentrate. The problem wasn't so much lack of practice or the foreign subject. She was overcome with inappropriate, if not indecent, feelings for the professor.

He never looked directly at her, but he gave no sign her presence bothered hm. He never glanced at his notes either. She couldn't believe how at ease he was, how professional. She was also amazed by the other students and the questions they asked. How did they know so much, understand so much? Most of them were geology majors and were genuinely interested in the subject.

After class, one of the students stopped to ask another question. She was eighteen or nineteen, slim and pretty, with short reddish-blonde hair, and her skirt barely covered her knees. She hugged her books to her small, firm breasts and fluttered her eyelashes as she asked her earnest question. She had pierced ears and wore too much perfume, a cheap, flowery scent.

Rynna got up slowly, walked to the desk, and stood a little to one side, waiting, not wanting to interrupt. As he answered the girl's question, Ted reached out and took Rynna's hand. The smile didn't falter, but the girl's gaze took in their joined hands and Rynna's maternity outfit. She thanked him and left.

He grinned. "Thanks."

"Don't you want sexy young girls to fall all over you?"

"No," he said. "I have enough trouble with you." He glanced toward the open door before he kissed her. "What did you think of mineralogy?"

"I'm overwhelmed," she said. "Will you help me with my homework?"

"Sure. But I can't help you with the tests, and I won't grade them." He squeezed her hand. "You don't have to do this," he said.

"I want to." She was a little shy with him now. She couldn't understand how someone who read as widely as he did and enjoyed such varied interests could be so deeply involved in a subject she found so dry and difficult. She wanted to understand it, wanted to like it, but it was impossible. Maybe she shouldn't try. She could concentrate on her own career, making a home for Ted and the baby. Still, she wanted to try. She wanted to be able to ask intelligent questions like the geology majors. She had a crush on her professor.

****

Rynna was even more overwhelmed in the lab section, but other students were equally lost. Ted was always patient with them. He had said he wouldn't want to teach her to drive because she didn't take direction well. Apparently, he didn't mind so much teaching her geology.

When he gave a lecture, he liked to sit on the desk, but in the lab, he stayed in the wheelchair so he could move freely among the students, who sat in pairs to share specimens. He took it so much for granted that they did the same. He talked to them casually, which they liked, but didn't court popularity. He didn't care if they liked him. He wanted them to learn the subject, and eventually, not without difficulty, most of them did.

After class, as she sat on a hard stone bench with her textbook, waiting for Ted, Rynna recognized one of her classmates among a trio of students who ambled past her and sat on the grass with their books and lunches. She glanced at them discreetly and returned to her reading. Yes, at least two of them carried the same book. She didn't want to eavesdrop, even less to identify herself. She grabbed her purse to leave.

"Too bad about Demeray," one young man said, and Rynna froze.

"He knows his stuff, though," countered another, and they moved on to discussing the assigned homework.

Did Ted know people said such things? Yes, of course he did. He was used to this attitude from strangers, and that might explain why he was so intolerant of it in those close to him. She wasn't used to it, and she wanted to hit out at them, but of course she couldn't. It would happen again, so she would have to learn to deal with it, but she must teach Robert never to pity anyone.

****

The following week Ted and Rynna found the house. They had examined mostly rentals, assuming a house worth buying would take longer and would have to wait. The important thing was to get out of Mrs. Katz's building and find a decent house with room for the baby. They started within walking distance of the university, but September was the wrong time of year in a college town, and not much was available.

River Valley Road was about three miles out. The quiet residential street ran for only five blocks and dead-ended near the river. Number 316 was for sale, but the owner had despaired of a suitable offer and decided to rent it for now and hope economic conditions would continue to improve.

The house was not impressive from the front, despite a new coat of white paint, and Rynna had little hope for it. The front lawn sloped slightly toward the street, and a flagstone pathway ended in a wide doorsill, flanked by unkempt bushes. No stairs at all—a definite plus. The window boxes and trite gingerbread trim were painted a woodsy dark green. If the house was big enough, it might do temporarily, but it was a long way from her dream house. She didn't want a Georgian mansion like Stonebridge, but the beauty of its lines and the quality of the wood and plasterwork had certainly spoiled her.

Inside the front door was a small entryway with a

large closet, and then they were in the living room. Rynna was ready with a dubious compliment, but she stopped and reconsidered. It had more light and space than she'd expected and high ceilings. The walls were freshly painted a pale green. Best of all were the built-in bookshelves and stone fireplace. This room at least she liked. She took Ted's hand but didn't glance at his face. No doubt he was reserving judgment, as he always did.

The dining room was small, but glass doors led onto the patio, so the light was good. If they entertained guests, the doors could be left open to extend the available space. The kitchen was all right too, with new tile and lots of cupboard space. Some of it was overhead, which wouldn't be convenient for Ted, but they would manage. She curbed her tendency to plan her life in every house she saw and tried the faucet above the sink to check the water pressure. The kitchen window let in a lot of light, too. The rooms would at least be cheerful on sunny days. Curtains would help, of course, and she might…but no, they wouldn't stay long in a house with forest-green shutters and gingerbread trim.

The three bedrooms were all good sizes, although she found it hard to judge without furniture. Two had built-in bookshelves and windows with double-hung sashes they could open in summer heat. The one on the street side would serve for Ted's study, and the quieter one at the end of the hall would make a lovely nursery, conveniently next to the master bedroom. So close to the river, they shouldn't need expensive air conditioning. She wandered from room to room and checked everything out, hunting for the catch. Ted and the realtor followed her, Ted in silence, the realtor carrying on a monologue neither of them listened to. The attached master bathroom was small, but the one off the hall was attractive and convenient with a big bathtub and sea green tile. It was not a perfect house, but…

She met Ted's gaze. "What do you think?" he asked. His tone was cool, reserved.

"It's nice." It was too weak a word, but nothing more precise came to mind.

"Let's look at the back yard," he said.

The covered patio was cool and pleasant, although the temperature was in the eighties. Beyond, a board fence enclosed an area of untended grass and two sturdy fruit trees. The gate between the front and back yards stood open, but they could lock it to make a safe place for the baby to play.

The garage adjoined the house, but with no connecting door. The space was enough for only one car, so one of them would have to park on the street or in the driveway. Rynna mentally listed all the disadvantages, but she had begun to want it anyway. It was unfurnished, but most of the furnished places had been dismal. She would have fun decorating it herself, but Ted might consider it too much trouble and expense.

The realtor rambled on about schools and convenience to shopping, and Ted interrupted him. "Rynna," he said, "do you want it?"

"Not if you don't like it," she hedged.

"Stop trying to be polite about everything. I can't read your mind. I can live anywhere. I want you to be happy."

"I *am* happy." She kissed him, ignoring the realtor.

They had a home.

Chapter Six

While they were eating dinner in the apartment breakfast nook, Rynna too excited to eat much and Ted indulging her need to chatter on about the house, the phone rang.

Ted answered curtly, "Yeah, Demeray."

Rynna picked at her spinach salad and watched him. She could tell nothing from his face.

"Yes," he said. "Yes, all right…No, it's fine…Yes." He hung up and rested his hand on the phone, his face revealing nothing.

"Who was it?"

He looked up, still expressionless. "Sergeant Chandler."

"Oh, no." Her heart sank. She had been so happy.

"He wants me to come in tomorrow."

"Just you? What does it mean?"

He shrugged. "We'll find out, I guess."

"I'll go with you."

"No, you won't. Let's not make a big deal out of this. He has a few more questions, that's all."

"I don't like this. I don't like Chandler."

"Rynna, don't worry. Don't think about it. Eat your dinner."

She couldn't eat. This was never going to end. Was there something new, some new evidence? What could it be? They had told the truth, most of it.

"Eat," Ted said and nudged her plate toward her. "Robert needs it, if you don't."

"I can't."

"Yes, you can," he said, but he didn't eat much himself.

What if the police didn't believe what they said? What if a jury didn't? They were innocent, but how did they prove it? Why was it only Ted they wanted to question again? What if he was sent to prison? What if...

"For God's sake, Rynna," he said. "Stop worrying. I'm not going to face a firing squad."

No, it would be the electric chair. Or, more likely, life in state prison. To tell the whole truth would make the situation worse. A jury wouldn't believe their story, but Ian Wyatt could testify *she* believed it. Her wonderful day, the day when they found their house, was ruined.

She slept fitfully and dreamed vividly of Jason's death. God damn you, Jason, she thought fiercely. You've done enough. Leave us alone.

****

In the morning, Ted gave Rynna half a dozen errands to run. He was only trying to keep her busy, but she was too choked with fear to argue. They had a lot to do if they were going to move into the house on River Valley Road. "I'll call you," he promised. "Don't worry."

She gave Mrs. Katz notice. She called the phone company. She picked up change-of-address forms at the post office. She kept her regular appointment with Dr. Moran. She worried.

Ted called while she was trying to eat lunch. She had managed to get the milk down, for Robert's sake, but her ham sandwich and apple were untouched. "Okay, it's over," he said. "Now will you stop worrying?"

"What happened?"

"I'll tell you about it later. I just have time to get to the lab." He hung up.

When he returned, she was studying her mineralogy textbook, bored but dutiful. He kissed her and took the book out of her hands. "No more homework," he said. "Let's go to a movie."

"Ted!" She smiled in spite of herself. They hadn't had a normal courtship, nothing she would have called a date. The only film they had ever watched together was about minerals.

"I'm serious," he said. "I'll let you choose. The new Hitchcock at the Palace, or we can go to the drive-in and neck."

"We can neck here."

"Too easy."

"I'd love to see a movie with you," she said. "But first tell me what happened this morning." She was greatly relieved. No doubt he was covering up, but she liked him in this mood. They couldn't be in immediate danger if he could tease her.

"More questions, mostly the same questions. He doesn't have anything, but he can't give up."

"What did you say?"

"Nothing new. Except he might have gotten the idea Jason had a hallucination, imagined he saw something."

"Oh, Ted that was clever…What aren't you telling me? He knows we got married."

"Yes, he mentioned it. You can't blame him. He can only see it as a motive for murder. He has a job to do. Now forget about it. Chandler has had enough of your attention today. Let's go out to dinner and a movie and talk about our house."

So they did—Italian food, *North by Northwest* at the Palace, and back to the apartment in a mood of romantic optimism. They would move to River Valley Road and live happily ever after. Rynna made hot chocolate, and they sat together on the sofa, talking quietly and kissing. Lulled, Rynna rested her head on his shoulder and fell silent, thinking of their future together.

"Rynna," he said, "do you miss…dancing and stuff like that?"

She raised her head, shocked. "Oh, sweetie, of course not."

He raised his eyebrows. "What does *that* mean?"

"It doesn't mean anything, or if it does it means I love you. I'm sorry if you don't like it, but I won't watch every word I say. I did enough of that with Jason."

"Yes, I'm sorry," he said. "I'm sure I make a lousy husband."

"I've had worse." He kissed her, half in apology, and she said, "You're very good at this anyway."

"You changed the subject," he complained.

"No, I didn't. I don't understand why you think dancing is such a big deal anyway. Jason never took me dancing after we were married, or only once. Most wives will tell you their husbands never take them dancing. It's a common complaint."

"I would."

"I bet you wouldn't. I'll make you a promise, though. If I ever feel deprived, I'll hold you to it. You'll have to take me to some ritzy place, and I'll dance with all the handsomest men in the room."

"Okay. Whatever makes you happy."

"You make me happy. You're all that's really important to me, Ted. You and Robert." He put his hand on her abdomen and kissed her again sweetly. "I remember the first time you did that," she said.

"Kissed you?"

"No." She put her hand on his. "This. Unwillingly."

"Not entirely, but you were Jason's wife then."

"And you were my cousin. What did you think of me when we first met?"

"Oh, very pretty, a definite Demeray look, but stuck up."

"I wasn't!"

"Yes, you were, or I thought you were, or wanted to. And ridiculously young and a lot of trouble. What did you think of me?"

"Rude, hateful, defensive. Intelligent. Off-limits."

He was nonplussed. Finally, he said, "You certainly didn't expect to end up like this."

"No, I didn't, but I saw through you after a while. I'm glad I stayed long enough. I'm glad we were friends first."

"I hope we'll always be friends."

"We will," she said. She tried to read his face. He loved her, and he knew she loved him now, but he wasn't ready to believe their relationship would last forever. Rynna, who had come a long way with him in a short time, was much more confident. She couldn't feel this safe if it wouldn't last. She was ready to be kissed, loved, cherished. "I'll never leave you," she said.

They made love with more than usual intensity, in defiance of the threat of Sgt. Chandler and in recognition of having nearly missed this entirely.

****

Rain fell steadily the day Ted and Rynna moved into 316 River Valley Road, which was an added inconvenience but didn't seem a bad omen. Everything was clean and fresh, and the parched lawn was already greener. The rain made a lovely, gentle, patter on the roof and against the windows, which reminded Rynna of her childhood and made it all the cozier.

They brought Ted's new desk from Mrs. Katz's and the elegant nursery furniture from Stonebridge, but everything else would be new. Much of the furniture had yet to be chosen, and the house echoed emptily even after everything was moved in. Half-furnished, but full of books, with no curtains except in the nursery, this was still home. They went wild at the supermarket—the big new refrigerator held so much more than the tiny one in the apartment. They didn't have enough dishes and silver to stock the cupboards, but Ted owned more than enough books. Every few minutes Rynna needed to add to her shopping list. Moving in was a little like camping out, sharing a wonderful adventure.

She brimmed with ideas and plans, things to buy, decorating decisions, creative enthusiasm. Ted, mildly amused, let her have her way in everything. He drew the line only when he thought she was taking on too much. "This doesn't all have to be done today," he said. "Take your time. Rest awhile, for God's sake."

"I don't need rest right now," she insisted. "You mustn't pamper me. It's good for me to be busy. Childbirth is work, you know. I have to keep in shape for it."

That silenced him, for a while at least.

She considered having the piano moved from Stonebridge but in the end decided to leave it in the music room. Although legally hers now, it still belonged to Rosalind. She could have shopped for a smaller piano with her own money. Ted shouldn't have to pay for it, even though his determination not to spend Grandmother's money had weakened a little with the newly discovered joys of buying things to please her. He had insisted he wouldn't spend the money on "things we don't need," and the basic principle was unshaken, but his perception of what they needed had changed. What he needed alone was minimal. What she and Robert needed was expanding daily.

****

The rain stopped sometime during the night, and Sunday was cool and sunny. Ted spent some time in the backyard and added gardening tools to the lengthening list of things they needed. They measured the living room windows for curtains, and Rynna said she might make them herself instead of trying to find exactly what she wanted.

"With all the projects you have in mind," he pointed out, handing her the tape measure, "you'll need help. Maybe we should hire a nurse for the baby."

Rynna stared at him. A nurse? On a professor's salary? Out of Grandmother's money? She couldn't imagine what he was thinking. Was he too used to the servants at Stonebridge? "Ted, I can raise my own child and do my own housework. I'm not helpless." She turned her back on him and headed down the hall to the bedroom they had chosen for his study. It was empty except for the desk and several unpacked boxes of books.

Ted came in behind her and picked up the conversation again. "I know you're not helpless. But I don't want you to wear yourself out, and you'll want to do other things."

"I know what it is," she said wisely. "You're afraid you'll be accused of expecting me to be just your wife."

He raised his eyebrows. "Something like that."

They made quick work of measuring the one window and crossed the hall to the master bedroom. Except for the nursery, this room was the closest to being finished. Rynna had already made up the bed with new linens and a double wedding ring quilt she had fallen in love with. Twin cherry nightstands held matching lamps, and the handsome dresser next to the door was half full of clothing. Only the dressing table, which would go against the wall next to the bathroom door, had yet to be delivered.

"I know you don't expect anything, so you're off the hook," she assured him. "This"—she gestured toward the windows with the measuring tape—"is what I want right now. If I want something else later on, I'll let you know. Trust me."

"All right, but if you decide you want to have an affair with one of my students, don't tell me."

"Oh, Ted!" She threw a pillow in his direction.

He did persuade her to sit for a while after lunch. She was behind on her mineralogy and determined not to use the house as an excuse to drop the class. Ted was making notes for his geochemistry lecture, so she dragged the rocking chair from the nursery into the study and labored over the bonding of crystals. While they were working in companionable silence, the doorbell rang.

Ted put down his pen, but she said, "Let me," glad to abandon the struggle. She got out of the rocking chair, not without difficulty, and went to answer the door. One of their new neighbors stood on the doorsill, a tall, big-boned woman in slacks, her sandy hair tied back with a scarf, a covered dish in her hands.

"Hi," she said breezily. "Just come over to welcome ya'll to the neighborhood. I won't stay, but I brought y'all a little somethin'."

"That's kind of you," Rynna said.

"I'm Fran Archer, by the way. Why, honey, just look at you. What are you doin', havin' twins?"

"No, I don't think so. I'm Rynna. Please come in for a minute." She said this with some trepidation. She wanted to be on friendly terms with the neighbors but was a little afraid this woman would be another Mrs. Katz. More good-natured, though—she could see that much.

"No, I won't stay. Wasn't invited, was I? I would like to meet your husband anyway. I guess he's your husband. The way you look he betta' be, right?"

Rynna laughed. She couldn't help it. Fran Archer's manner was too warm to be offensive. "Have a seat," she said, gesturing toward the cluttered couch. "I'll put this in the kitchen. It was so kind of you to think of us."

"That's what neighba's are for, right?" Fran didn't sit and looked around eagerly. "Why, honey, y'all are fixin' this up real nice. The Thayers who lived here before ya'll were good folks, you know, but no imagination. I can see y'all have a real flair." She gave the word two syllables. The living room was a shambles, the dining room set hadn't been delivered, and nothing was finished, so this was more than kind. Fran followed Rynna into the kitchen and exclaimed again, although they had added nothing except the newly installed telephone and a few inexpensive kitchen towels. "This is all gonna be real nice."

Ted appeared in the doorway in his wheelchair. He looked the way he had before the first mineralogy class—braced for something but looking forward to it. "Fran, this is my husband, Ted Demeray."

"Hello, honey," Fran drawled, smiling broadly. "You folks sure are fixin' things up real nice here. I see y'all are plannin' on a little addition, too. My lord, I believe it's been ten years since we had a baby on the block. It's gonna be real nice having y'all here. I'm Fran Archer, by the way, from next door, you know. Just brought y'all a little something by way of welcome. I won't stay but a minute. Wasn't invited, was I?"

"Very glad to meet you," he said, as soon as he had a chance.

"I won't stay. I know you folks are busy. Bring the dish back when you're finished with it. No rush at all, give us a chance to say hello again. George—that's my husband—he's not up to visitin' today, but he'll be glad to see y'all any time you come by."

"I hope he isn't ill," Rynna said.

"No, no, honey, he's a little low today is all. Hard on a man gettin' old, you know. He's recently retired. That's all that ails him. Be good for him to see young folks like y'all." She grinned at Ted. "Younger folks yet to come, too. You sure she isn't havin' twins, honey?"

"Jesus, I hope not," he said.

"Hope not," Fran echoed. "Twice the work, twice the joy. You take good care of her now, honey. When do you think it's gonna be?"

"Not 'til December," Rynna told her. "Around Christmas, I think."

"That would be real nice, honey. Real nice. A

Christmas baby. That would be simply the best. Listen, I know you folks are busy, so I won't stay."

Rynna, bracing herself, said, "I could make some coffee and offer you some of this." She lifted the cover to reveal a luscious chocolate cake.

"No, no, honey, too much chocolate doesn't agree with me, and if I drink another cup of coffee today, I'll slosh. I won't stay, but it sure was nice to meet you folks." She backed out of the kitchen, still talking. "Come on over any time. We're always home. Don't wait to be invited. Just barge in like I did. If y'all need to borrow a cup of sugar or anything, don't hesitate. That's what neighba's are for, right?"

"Yes. Thank you."

"Real pleased to meet you both. 'Bye now."

When she was gone, Rynna met Ted's eyes, and they both laughed.

"It was kind of her," she said. "I liked her. I couldn't help it."

"Yes, I liked her too," he said, "but I don't much like being called honey by a perfect stranger."

"You don't like your own wife calling you honey," Rynna reminded him. She sighed over the chocolate cake. "So much for my diet."

"Come here, honey," Ted said. He took her hand, and she bent to kiss him. He more than responded and then grinned. "That was real nice," he said.

"Young folks like us," she quoted. "Did you hear what she said when she first came in? You'd better be my husband, the way I look."

He sobered. "You're not going to have twins, are you?"

"Of course not. We'd know by now. She was

exaggerating."

Ted didn't answer. He put both hands on her belly, and she covered his with hers. A silent, peaceful interlude, the two of them united in perfect intimacy.

"What are you thinking?" she asked.

He didn't answer at once. "I wish you didn't have to go through all this," he said.

"Sweetie, are you still worried? Having a baby is wonderful. It's something I've always wanted. The problems your mother had are rare."

"I know," he said, "but—"

"Please don't, Ted. I do understand, but please let me enjoy having this baby."

"I'm sorry. I don't understand why you aren't scared."

"Why should I be? I'm strong and healthy. The baby is fine."

"But it's your first baby. How do you know? How can you be so confident?"

"I don't know, but it feels perfectly natural and simple to me. It's an incredible feeling to have a baby grow inside you. I wish I could make you understand." She gave up, frustrated. Every woman faced this to some degree. His problem wasn't so much that Clara had nearly died in childbirth as that he didn't know what it was like to be pregnant, and she couldn't tell him.

****

That night, after they made love for the first time in their new house, they lay together in comfortable silence and listened to the light patter of rain on the window. Ted had one arm around Rynna, her head on his shoulder, and the other hand, as so often, rested lightly on her abdomen. She couldn't understand how he could be apprehensive about what was happening to her and yet find the changes in her body physically appealing. "You're funny," she said, putting her hand on his. "Will you still love me when I'm flat again?"

"I expect so."

She was silent again for a while, and then she said, "I wonder if you do love me." He didn't answer and waited for her to continue. "I don't want to be the kind of wife who needs to be reassured all the time, but I wouldn't mind being told once in a while. I don't believe you've said, 'I love you' half a dozen times."

He said nothing, unwilling to let her tease or provoke him.

"I think the last time was before we were married," she said. "Now you take me for granted."

"Rynna," he said patiently, "would I put up with you if I didn't love you?"

She had to laugh. "No, I guess not. Do you know what I wish?"

He brushed her hair back from her face. "What do you wish?"

"I wish the baby would look like you."

"For God's sake. Why?"

"A boy should look like his father."

"I'm not—" he said and caught himself. He had asked her not to say those words. "Wouldn't you rather he was good-looking?"

"Yes, I would rather he was terribly attractive. I would like him to have blond hair and a slight cleft in his chin. And you have beautiful eyes."

He ignored the compliments. "Pamela was blonde."

"Yes. He might look like my mother." She wished she believed it. She was afraid he would look exactly like his biological father.

"All I want is…I don't want anything to happen to you or the baby."

"Nothing will happen, Ted."

He took her face in his hands and kissed her. "See that it doesn't," he said. "I love you."

Chapter Seven

Rynna dreamed she was back at Stonebridge, sitting on the staircase with its dark, polished banisters. Jason lay on the hardwood floor where he'd fallen. The sickening thud his body had made still echoed in her ears. He stirred and began to rise, and she watched, choked with horror.

She couldn't scream, couldn't get her breath. Ted was upstairs somewhere, but even if she could make a sound, he couldn't come quickly enough.

Jason was standing now, shaking his head to clear it. Blood glistened on his head and his hands, but he didn't appear to be seriously hurt. He spotted her on the stairs and approached her. She couldn't move.

"I've had about enough shit from you," he said, his face dark with anger. Blood dripped from his hair, down his face. He brushed it out of his eyes.

"Jason, please," she managed to whisper. She rose, backed against the banister. She couldn't have climbed the stairs to save her life. Jason stood over her and took her by the throat, blood on his hands, dripping into his eyes. She was sure she was going to faint. He kissed her, an ugly, brutal kiss, and his breath stank of corruption. He held her throat tightly with one hand and lowered the other to her belly.

"This is mine," he said harshly. "I take what is mine." He put his mouth on hers again, and she tasted blood. She gagged, choked, tried again to scream.

She woke, trembling, her heart pounding. She must have screamed after all, and Ted was awake, holding her. "It's all right," he said. "It was only a dream." She was in their comfortable new house, not at Stonebridge.

Only a dream, but horrible, so horrible. "Jason," she said, trying to tell him. "He…"

"I know," he said, "but it's over. You're safe now."

She didn't feel safe, not yet. She was trembling, sobbing. Ted murmured softly, comforting her. He stroked her hair, her face, and she relaxed a little, but she tensed up when he tried to kiss her. "Shh," he said. "You're all right now. You're here with me. Jason is dead."

"No," she said, fighting for breath. "He…"

"It was a dream, Rynna. It's over now. Don't cry." He brushed the tears away and touched her face gently, lovingly. He kissed the angle of her jaw, and his fingers brushed her throat.

"No!" She pulled away, choked, terrified. "Don't, please don't."

"I'm sorry," he said. He drew back. "I won't touch you if you don't want me to."

She finally grew calmer and caught her breath. "It was horrible," she said. "Jason was alive, but all bloody."

"Jesus," he said.

Rynna took refuge, more instinctively than willingly, in his arms. "Hold me," she said, "but don't kiss me. I feel…polluted."

"Rynna!"

"Please hold me." He held her, and she relaxed, comforted. But she hadn't told him the worst. What did Jason mean? *I take what is mine.*

She did sleep, but when she faced the mirror in the morning, the evidence suggested otherwise. She had dark circles under her eyes. It wasn't only a figure of speech, then. She did what she could with cold water and makeup, so Ted wouldn't notice. How many times had she done this in the past, to erase the signs of Jason's violence? Sometimes she had fooled Ted.

This time wasn't much of a success. She came out of the bathroom, and as soon as he saw her face, he said, "Jesus, Rynna."

"I know I look awful, but I'm all right." She patted his arm to reassure him.

"You look like hell. Were you sick?"

She hesitated. She could easily blame her pregnancy, but no, he would worry about that too. "No, it's just lack of sleep. The dream." A stab of horror passed through her at the memory, and she looked away. "I'll take a nap later."

He was still watching her, still worried.

"I'm sorry I'm so much trouble," she said. She remembered that she hadn't let him kiss her afterward, had backed away when he touched her throat, overcome by the vivid images of the dream. She kissed him. "I'll make breakfast."

"I can do it," he said.

"I know, but I'd rather." She kissed him again and left him sitting on the bed, still disturbed.

She did take a nap after lunch and a long walk in the fresh air, and by the time Ted came home from the university she looked as well as she felt. She told him what she'd accomplished in the house, and after a while he stopped watching her so closely and relaxed.

He was, as always, agreeable about helping her with

80

the housework. She was surprised he could have lived at Stonebridge for years, taking servants for granted, and yet help her clear the table after dinner as a matter of course. She washed the dishes, and he dried them. He stood to put the plates away in the overhead cupboard, and Rynna caught her breath. "Quit showing off," she said to cover her concern.

He closed the cupboard door. "Come here," he said, and she went willingly into his arms. The last time she had stood with him like this was right after Jason had fallen to his death. In spite of that vivid memory, she liked the size of him in her arms. He was almost as tall as Jason and broader through the shoulders. All the years of pushing those wheels had developed his chest and arm muscles, as Jason had found to his cost.

"Lovely," she said, nestling. He took her face in his hands and kissed her lingeringly. "Now you really are showing off," she said as soon as she could breathe.

"You talk too much," he said and kissed her again.

"Ted! You shouldn't kiss me like that in the kitchen."

"We could sit on the sofa and neck," he suggested.

"Don't you have work to do?"

"Not tonight." He kissed her again, and she struggled to think straight. She had been able to tell from the way Jason kissed her when he wanted sex, but he had never been able to stir her own desire like this.

"We could go to bed, then," she said.

"A little early, isn't it?"

"We're newlyweds," she reminded him.

They were in the bedroom, Rynna half out of her skirt, when the phone rang. "Damn," she said. Ted left to answer it, and she remembered another time when they were happy until the phone rang. She hoped Sgt. Chandler hadn't called again.

Ted was gone for a long time. At first Rynna sat on the bed in her slip and waited for him, but she soon became annoyed, resentful. What could be so goddamned important? She put her clothes back on and went into the nursery. The room was cheerful and calming, a symbol of all her hopes for the future. She should hem the curtains or work on the wretched afghan. What was he talking about?

When he returned, she was sitting on the bed again, pretending to read her mineralogy text. He took the book out of her hands and kissed her. "Sorry," he said.

"Who was it?" she asked, a little sulky.

"Just business," he said. "Sorry about the timing."

"Just business?" She was furious. "What business? Are you keeping secrets from me now? *More* secrets I should say."

"Hey." He sat close and put his arm around her, but she resisted. "Rynna!" He was half amused, not understanding.

"Don't use that tone with me," she snapped. "You think you know everything. You think I'm stupid." She grabbed the textbook and threw it at the wall. "You and your horrible rocks. You—you goddamned Demeray."

"Hey," he said again and pulled her close. "Give me a break," he said against her hair. "I'm sorry if I was evasive. I'll tell you about it, all right?"

"You'd better," she said sulkily.

"I will, and you don't have to study those horrible rocks. I never asked you to."

"I know you didn't. I didn't mean that. I was—"

"I know. You are more of a Demeray than I am, you

know."

"Technically, anyway." She relaxed in his arms. "Tell me who called."

"You remember Norris and Osborn?"

"Yes." Of course she did. The night they came to dinner, she had pleaded exhaustion, certain she would break apart if Jason laid a finger on her. Two days later he was dead. She knew Ted wasn't thinking about the same thing. "You mean they're still trying to buy the mineral rights?"

"Yes. They have another lawyer now."

"And…"

"And we have a lawyer. Two lawyers, in fact."

"You're still going to fight them? With Grandmother's money? Is it…is it dangerous?"

"Dangerous? It's not dangerous. It's just boring, a lot of legal nonsense."

"But if they know you're trying to stop them—"

"They're not gangsters, Rynna. They don't hire hit men. It's all legal maneuvering."

"Are you sure?"

"Yes, I'm sure. Are you satisfied, or do you want to hear all the boring details?"

"You think everything you do will bore me."

"Doesn't it?"

"Yes. But once I get the hang of it, I might like geology. I'm sorry about the book. Was it good news or bad news? You can tell me that much without putting me to sleep, can't you?"

"Neither one." He was evasive again, and she raised her chin, ready to fight. "Mostly bad, I guess," he said, heading her off. "It's not something we can settle overnight. It'll be a long fight."

"And expensive?"

"Yes. Do you mind?"

"Why should I? It's your money."

"Eventually it'll be Robert's."

She hadn't thought of that. "Why didn't you tell me?"

"Don't you have enough to think about?"

"Yes. Don't you? Why are you still—?"

"Don't you want me to fight them? They'll tear up the valley."

"Yes, of course they should be stopped, but I didn't know you cared about this. I thought it was because Jason was involved."

"No, it wasn't." But of course it was, at least in the beginning. If anything happened, if any trouble arose from this…Jason already had a great deal to answer for.

Rynna no longer wanted to make love. The delay and the loss of mood didn't help, and now Jason's name had once again been spoken. She was on the edge of despair. He would never leave them in peace.

****

Rynna dreamed of Stonebridge again. She sat on the stairs as before, and Jason lay dead in the hall. She didn't know where Ted was. Jason struggled to his feet. He was stunned, groggy, his vision unclear. He shook his head, swayed a little, and touched his forehead. His fingers came away with blood on them. "Bastards," he muttered. He glanced around but didn't see her on the stairs. He stood still a little longer, a bit unsteady on his feet, and then he advanced slowly, but with purpose, toward the door.

He walked right through it. The door was closed and securely locked, and he marched through it without hesitation. He was dead, after all.

She woke feeling frightened, but not as badly as the previous night. The dream was scary, and she was sick of Jason, dead or alive, but he hadn't seen her, hadn't touched her. A dream was not reality.

She didn't want to wake Ted just because she'd had a dream and was frightened. She wasn't a child. She was going to have a child of her own. If Robert had bad dreams and woke in the dark, she would be the strong, wise parent who would comfort him and kiss away his tears.

"Rynna?" Ted stirred, reached for her hand. "What's wrong?"

"Nothing," she whispered. "It was only a dream."

"Jason?"

"Yes. It's all right." She snuggled closer, unsure whether she wanted to soothe him or to seek comfort.

"Are you sure?" he asked sleepily.

"I'm sure. Go to sleep. I love you."

In the morning, the sun was shining, and everything was as it should be. While Ted shaved, Rynna headed for the kitchen to put the coffee on.

The front door was standing open.

She stared, unable to make sense of what she was seeing. Ted had locked the door last night. She was sure of it. She glanced around the living room, the kitchen, out the dining room doors to the patio and the yard beyond. Nobody was there. Nothing was missing.

She returned to the door. Nothing suggested forced entry, no marks on the door or the lock. She put her hand on the closet door but couldn't will herself to open it. How silly. Nobody would have come into the house during the night and taken nothing, disturbed nothing.

The lock must be defective. If the door was unlatched, the wind might have blown it the rest of the way. They would simply have the lock fixed.

Nobody was hiding in the closet. She could open the door to show herself how foolish she was to think so. She took her hand off the knob and backed away. If she told Ted, he would have the lock changed. He would check the closet to be sure. He was matter-of-fact, a scientist. He wouldn't be afraid to investigate. Why was she afraid? Why did she sense somebody was in the house?

She took hold of the closet doorknob again. Robert stirred and kicked her. "Hush," she said, putting her hands to her belly.

Ted came up behind her. "Rynna," he said. "What—?"

She jumped. "Look, the door was open."

He closed it firmly. They heard a small click, and it swung slightly open again. "I'll be damned," he said. He opened the closet door and glanced in. He didn't see anything, of course. "Nothing missing?" he asked.

"No. At least I couldn't tell. You have so many books."

"Which nobody would want to steal."

"No," she agreed, with a shaky laugh.

"Were you scared?"

"Not really." She kissed him warmly. He did have a knack for coming through when she needed him.

"What was that for?"

"I'll think of something."

He returned to the problem at hand, predictably practical. "I'll call a locksmith to put in a deadbolt."

While they were eating breakfast, he asked, "Did you sleep better last night?"

"Much. I had another dream, but it was just eerie. You mustn't worry about any of this, Ted. It'll pass."

"I hope so."

"Don't you ever dream about...about the night Jason died?"

"Not after the first couple of days."

"What *do* you dream about?"

He took her hand. "You."

****

A locksmith duly replaced the lock on the front door, and the house was secure. But something lingered after the incident, a superstition about the entryway and especially the coat closet next to the door. Rynna avoided it, hesitated to open the door. It was foolish, and she didn't mention her squeamishness to Ted. She had scoffed at Lucy's unwillingness to enter the music room at Stonebridge. This was the same thing and every bit as illogical.

She didn't dream again of Jason or Stonebridge, but sometimes, when she was alone, she had a feeling somebody else was in the house. She didn't feel threatened or even frightened, but she was a little uneasy, as if someone waited near the front door. She didn't tell Ted. She didn't know what he would say, but she knew what Ian Wyatt would've said. She ought to be committed.

She baked raisin oatmeal cookies for the Archers and took them next door with the empty cake dish. She had eaten only one cookie, but she understood why so many housewives struggled with their weight. At Stonebridge, where she'd never had to lift a finger to have good hot meals, she had eaten well, but never gained weight until she got pregnant. She hadn't had the temptation to taste and snack during the day as she did when she prepared meals herself.

Fran answered the doorbell with her hair in curlers and an apron tied around her waist. "Hello, honey, come on in."

"I don't want to bother you if you're doing your housework. I wanted to bring back your dish, and I made cookies, so I brought you some."

"Now, that's real nice, honey. They look wonderful. Come right on in. Don't mind the mess. I was just washin' up the breakfast dishes. Come on in and keep me comp'ny for a while."

The house wasn't a mess. The living room was neater than Rynna's and not only because Ted's books were still everywhere. She followed Fran into the large, spotless kitchen. Seated at the table with a newspaper spread out before him was an overweight, gray-haired, unshaven man in his sixties.

"This is my husband, George," Fran explained unnecessarily. "George, this is our little neighba' from next door. She's brought us some raisin cookies, wasn't that sweet?"

Rynna held out her hand, ignoring the scent of unwashed socks, and George took it solemnly. "I'm Rynna Demeray," she said.

"Pleased ta meetcha," he said with grave sincerity.

"Sit down, honey," Fran said. "Take a load off your feet. I know what it's like carryin' a baby." Rynna perched on the nearest chair, across the table from George. "We have two kids, all grown up now, of course. George, have some of these cookies. They look real good."

George took two cookies, demolished the first in

two bites, and said, "Real good."

Fran, her hands in soapy water, talked nonstop about the weather, the neighborhood, and her own recipe for raisin cookies. George gave Rynna a thin smile of commiseration. Something else was in his eyes, something like hunger. Fran interrupted herself to ask Rynna if she wanted a cup of coffee.

"No, thank you. I'll have to get back in a minute. I still have so much to do."

"Oh, I know, honey. There's never any end to it, is there? You should see what they're doin' over there, George. It's gonna be real nice. Y'all have enough books to start a library, don't you?"

"Yes. They're all Ted's."

"What does he do, honey? I don't rememba' if you told me."

Rynna suppressed a laugh. When had she had a chance to tell Fran anything? "He teaches at the university. The geology department."

"That's real nice," Fran enthused. "A good profession, teachin', and now you'll have a nice little family. That's real nice."

Into the brief silence while she dried her hands, smiling at Rynna, George said, "Damn shame."

"What is, George?" Fran asked, her tone gently humoring. She glanced at him, as if expecting him to point out something in the newspaper.

"Pretty young girl like her," he said. "Spend her life pushin' a wheelchair."

"Now, George."

Rynna was too stunned to answer at first, and then she said, stumbling a little over the words, "But I don't."

"Leave her be, George," Fran said.

"I don't," Rynna said. She wanted him to understand. "I never have. He wouldn't let me." She stood, and Fran looked vaguely alarmed.

"Sit down, honey. Don't pay any mind to George."

"He's perfectly capable of doing it himself," Rynna said to George. "He's stronger than I am."

George stared at the newspaper. "Damn shame," he said again, but with less conviction. He grabbed another cookie.

Fran patted Rynna's arm. "Now, you mustn't let George upset you, honey. He doesn't mean anything. Sit down, and I'll get you a cup of coffee."

"No, thank you. I'd better go. You've been very kind."

She returned to her own small, warm kitchen—a little cluttered, but hers—and burst into tears.

The incident was one more thing she didn't tell Ted. She told him about meeting George and described him and his conversational style but didn't report everything he said.

"You're holding out on me," Ted said at once. "What did he say?"

She shook her head. "It was nothing."

"Let me guess. You'll have to toughen up."

"I know," she said. "I knew you'd say that. I will. I'll learn." She was glad he didn't know she had cried about it.

Chapter Eight

The next week Rynna bought a car. She wouldn't drive Jason's Ferrari. She would sell it and add the money to Ian's inheritance. She assumed her own car should be a station wagon, suitable for hauling children and groceries, but Ted said she should have whatever she wanted. His car was practical—good mileage and plenty of room in the back for the wheelchair—but it was also what he wanted.

What she wanted, after she considered the models she should choose and returned to it again and again, was a flashy red Thunderbird.

Ted was amused. "That's a very fancy car," he told her.

"But expensive."

"It's a good car, though. There's a seat belt option, so it should be safe."

"It's too small, isn't it? It wouldn't be practical."

"It's not bad. It'll be years before the kids will be big enough for us to need a station wagon."

"The kids?" she repeated, raising her eyebrows.

"Yes," he said. "The kids."

They bought the Thunderbird. She loved it. When she drove it, she felt adventurous and had to remind herself Ted would never let her forget it if she earned a speeding ticket.

Despite the intermittent rain, the weather stayed

warm well into October, and the cool, sheltered patio was more than welcome. Ted used the riding mower, filling the air with the fresh, pungent odor of newly mown grass, and the yard began to look, as Fran would've said, "real nice."

One fine evening they sat on the patio after dinner, Ted with a book as usual and Rynna halfheartedly working at her baby afghan. She had been crocheting forever, with little result. She had been working on it the day in the library—how many months ago?—when Ted, busy with Grandmother's books, casually mentioned his adoption. She gazed at him, remembering. How incredible that they had come this far and were lawfully married.

"What are you thinking?" he asked, without glancing up from his book. He could feel her gaze on him.

"Nothing much," she said.

Dry leaves crunched underfoot, and George Archer shuffled through the open gate. "Evenin'," he said. He wore rumpled slacks and a dirty undershirt but had shaved recently.

"Hello," Rynna said, keeping her voice steady.

He bobbed his head briefly at Ted. "George'rcher," he said.

"Yes. I'm Ted. We met your wife the other day."

George gave Rynna his thin smile. "Talker," he said.

"It's going to cool off now, I think," Ted said.

George glanced around the yard and turned back to Ted. "Korea?"

"No. Arthritis. Have you and Fran lived here long?"

George sighed. "Twenty years." He lingered a little longer, not looking at either of them, said, "Evenin'," again, and shuffled back the way he had come.

Those weeks passed quickly, filled with work and love and laughter. Fran Archer gave Rynna a baby shower and invited the other women in the neighborhood, so she met them all and felt included.

She met Ted's colleagues and their wives at her first faculty tea. He had offered her the out of pleading advanced pregnancy, but she would have to face it sooner or later. The baby at least gave people something to say in the first awkward moments, but the formal affair was much more of an ordeal than the baby shower. She was aware of a certain amount of coolness, of rude stares and whispered remarks broken off when she approached. They knew who she was—the shameless woman who might have murdered her first husband and who had remarried with indecent haste. If the women of River Valley Road knew anything about Jason's death, they gave no sign. She much preferred them to these stuffy faculty wives.

Although she didn't mean to, she further alienated them when one of the older professors introduced the subject of desegregation. At Stonebridge, although the Demerays read the newspapers, they were isolated, removed from the world of politics, but here "massive resistance" was urgent business. Rynna had grown up in an all-white neighborhood, and Colorado hadn't yet integrated its schools in response to *Brown v. Board of Education*, but her college classes had been more diverse, and she'd had a history professor who spoke eloquently about Little Rock. She wanted to ask, "What are you so afraid of?" but settled for asking why the prospect of desegregation was so terrible. Everyone within earshot reacted with astonished horror.

Ted had grown up here and was used to this mindset, but when she turned to him for support, he squeezed her hand and said mildly, "I think it's time."

They didn't like his response either, but he was a Virginia native, a wealthy Demeray, and a respected professor, and he didn't care about currying favor with them. The coolness only increased with his outsider wife.

At least Ted didn't expect her to entertain the faculty wives at home. He did invite Fred Sullivan, and she liked him a lot after she overcame her shyness in the face of his authority. He was the department head, but he was Ted's friend first. Don Casper visited a few times, too, and he was one of the funniest men she had ever met. He didn't tell jokes. He claimed not to know any. But everything he said was funny, part of his distorted view of life. He had been paralyzed in a car accident and was a skilled and experienced wheelchair athlete.

A more frequent visitor was Ted's teaching assistant, Elaine Lockwood, a neat, trim, sensible woman about Rynna's age. At first Rynna was as wary of her as of his female students, convinced they were all her rivals. She envied Elaine's self-confident manner and her effortless understanding of the subject. When Elaine and Ted talked to each other, they might have been speaking a foreign language. He could easily tire of trying to explain geology to Rynna and spend long evenings in his tiny university office with Elaine, drifting from deep discussion to deeper intimacy, while his ignorant wife grew fatter and crankier.

In fact, he seemed scarcely aware Elaine was a woman. She was a colleague. She worked hard and knew her stuff, and he could rely on her. He never called her anything but "Lockwood" in an offhand, yet courteous way, and she treated him with teasing respect. He was, she told Rynna, the best she had ever worked with and always helpful with her own studies, and she wasn't about to jeopardize her position.

She very quickly became Rynna's closest friend, someone she could confide in, woman to woman, when Ted wouldn't understand. She could tell her when she was hurt by thoughtless, slighting remarks. "Listen," Elaine said, in the same matter-of-fact tone she used to discuss geology with Ted. "Don't let anybody tell you what to feel, least of all Demeray. Geology he knows. Women? Forget it."

Even as she eased Rynna's fear of these people who knew so much more than she did, she revealed her own frank, wistful envy of Rynna's condition. She wanted a baby more than she wanted her PhD, which was quite a lot. She did not, however, want any of the men she'd considered as possible husbands. The baby would have to wait. Sharing Rynna's confidences was as close as she would come for now.

Elaine was the one who told her about the childbirth preparation class offered on campus. Rynna discussed the possibility of natural childbirth with Dr. Moran and read *Childbirth Without Fear* by Grantly Dick-Read and the popular new book on the Lamaze method. She was still undecided, but Elaine assured her she could go to the classes and keep all her options open.

Dr. Moran wasn't going to deliver the baby. He continued to see her regularly but also referred her to Dr. Zalman, the obstetrician who would attend the birth. Dr. Zalman was strongly in favor of Dr. Dick-Read's methods and assured Rynna that anything that helped her feel more relaxed or more confident would make labor easier and give the baby a better start.

She was grateful that the university community, although backward in race relations, was progressive enough to have a teaching hospital that embraced such radical ideas as fathers in the labor room. She explained that and more to Ted on the first cool evening of fall in front of a crackling fire, the first in their new house.

He was skeptical. "Are you giving me a pep talk?" he asked.

"Yes."

"Why?"

"I thought you might like to go to class with me."

"I don't even want to think about this."

"I know. That's why you should go. The more you understand, the less scary it is. It doesn't commit you to anything, Ted. If you take the full course, Dr. Zalman will let you be with me in the labor room, but—"

"Jesus, Rynna."

"Don't panic. I didn't say you had to. But if you don't take the classes, they won't let you. I won't push you into anything, I promise, but it might be easier for you to be involved, or at least informed, than to sit in the waiting room and imagine things. It's your decision, but I would like you to be there."

"In the labor room?"

She laughed at his expression.

He looked into the flames and after a moment took her hand in both of his but said nothing more.

"Just think about it," she said.

She gave him the book Dr. Moran had recommended, and he spent another quiet evening reading it and then gave it back. "Rynna, did you read this? All of it?"

"Yes. Why?"

"It's hair-raising. I'll go to class with you, but don't give me any more books."

So Rynna added the childbirth classes to the rest of her projects. Ted thought she did too much, but she could cite any one of several authorities—Dr. Moran, Dr. Zalman, Chrissy Hartman, the midwife who conducted the classes—to support her arguments. She was better off being busy, active. She thrived on it. She was happy.

But when she was alone in the house, she sometimes sensed an alien presence. Somebody was waiting. Sometimes, when she was unnerved, she left the house, took a stroll or visited Fran or Mrs. Trask, the neighbor on the other side.

Fran dropped in and appraised her redecorating progress. "It's all real nice, honey." Ted had transferred some of his books to his university office, but the shelves were still too full. Some were now in boxes in the garage, though, and the house bore less resemblance to a publisher's warehouse.

One morning, as she browsed through the newspaper after Ted left for his geochemistry class, she came across an article about the mysterious ailment that had killed William Jr. She wasn't worried about it—she didn't think so anyway—but she hoped Ted hadn't seen it. He had read the paper, so it was too late to hide it. She threw it away, so he couldn't be tempted to peruse it again. Later she reminded herself she shouldn't try to protect him. He couldn't protect her from being hurt either. Life was sometimes hard. She needed to toughen up.

****

After her doctor's appointment, Rynna ambled back

to the car, window-shopping. She had parked the Thunderbird half a mile away for the exercise, but she wasn't in the mood for a brisk walk. Thanksgiving was a few weeks away, and the store windows were bright with autumn displays. Nearly every one held something she wanted to stop and examine. She had to constantly restrain herself from buying anything more for the baby. In addition to the layette she'd begun to accumulate as early as her second month and the baby shower gifts, Elaine kept finding clothing she "just couldn't resist." Robert would be an exceptionally well-dressed child.

She thought ahead to Christmas instead—their first Christmas together. Last year she had been on her honeymoon with Jason, and they had spent Christmas with his Wyatt cousins, a cheerful family Christmas, unshadowed by what was to come. Ted was alone at Stonebridge. She ought to make up for it now. Next year Robert would be old enough to enjoy the excitement, if not to understand. This year was special; this year she and Ted would lay the foundations of their own family traditions. Their plans were provisional, of course, as her official due date was Christmas Eve. Everybody told her to put no stock in an arbitrary date, though. "Babies," Dr. Zalman assured her, "come when they are ready."

She wanted to buy something special for Ted, which was no easy task. He didn't want anything. He was increasingly generous about buying things for the house, for her, or for Robert, but he didn't want anything for himself. Books were the only possessions he valued, and he owned more than enough.

She was happy. If her biggest concern was what to give him for Christmas, how could she not be happy? She was making an attractive, comfortable home for the man she loved and the child they would have. She had managed to earn a C+ on her mineralogy midterm, and she *had* earned it. Elaine didn't give her the slightest benefit of the doubt. She had made friends in this new world, people she could rely on. Ted remained her best friend and, although he wouldn't often say so, he loved her.

Half a block from the car, she glanced away from the drugstore window where an aftershave display spilled out of a cornucopia and spotted a man in a wheelchair. Not Ted, of course, an older man with one leg amputated above the knee, but she found herself taking a second glance, and smiled to herself, as she sometimes did when she encountered a young man with blond hair and glasses. My God, she thought, I am *so* in love.

When she got home empty-handed, having resisted every temptation, she rewarded herself with a raisin cookie—Fran's recipe—and a glass of milk for Robert's sake. While she was in the kitchen, she heard something and went to investigate. She didn't find anything. Nothing in the living room, nothing in the hall. She didn't check the closet. She had thrown her coat across the bed rather than hang it up. "This is stupid," she said aloud and put her hand on the doorknob, but she couldn't force herself to twist it. She thought of Ted, how he would tease her if he knew. She should open the door to prove she wasn't afraid. She was harboring a superstition, a foolish fantasy.

In the end she decided she didn't have to prove anything to anybody and returned to the kitchen. Perversely, the feeling grew stronger. She didn't have anything to fear in its well-lit space, but if she went out, someone would surely be lurking in the hall. Had Ted asked Elaine to handle the lab and come home early? Or Fran Archer…

No. Somebody was waiting. Waiting, watching.

Someone who did not wish them well.

****

When Ted got home, she was busy with dinner, the kitchen warm and filled with the rich odors of pot roast and gravy. He didn't need to know she'd skipped her nap because she was afraid to go to sleep alone in the house. All he needed to know was that she was, as always, glad to see him and dinner was in the oven. He didn't ask what she was cooking. He was easy to please or impossible to please, depending on how she considered the question. The way to his heart wasn't through his stomach.

He told her about his day and then asked, "Did you see Phil Moran today?"

"Yes." She gathered silverware from the drawer to set the table, and he took them from her. "He said we should wait now."

He laid knives and forks on the table and said, "I thought he might."

Rynna put her arms around his shoulders from behind. It was hard to get close now, with her belly in the way. "Do you mind?" she asked, a silly question with no acceptable answer. Wisely, he didn't try.

In bed that night he kissed her mouth with unusual restraint and said, "Turn over. I'll rub your back."

She lay on her side and he gently, expertly, massaged her spine exactly where it did the most good. "Lovely," she murmured. She could easily fall asleep like this. Instead, her thoughts strayed to the events of the day and the creepy sensation she'd had earlier. The feeling was gone now, as it always was when Ted was home. It was nothing but a reaction to being alone.

"You're tensing up," Ted said. "Relax."

She relaxed. After a while she asked, "What are you thinking about?"

He hesitated. "I'm not going to tell you."

"Rocks," she guessed. How unflattering. She rolled onto her back and settled next to him, ready for sleep, which didn't come.

"What are *you* thinking about?" he asked, aware of her stubborn wakefulness.

"Sex," she said. "After the baby is born, I'll have stretch marks and two o'clock feedings, and you won't want me anyway."

"Fat chance," he said. "And we can take turns with the two o'clock feedings."

"You are good to me," she said warmly. They were silent for a long time and then, sensing he was still awake, she said, "Ted?"

"Hmm?"

"Speaking of sex—"

"Which we weren't."

"After the baby is born, we'll have to think about birth control. I think the easiest thing would be for me to ask Dr. Zalman to tie my tubes when he delivers the baby. It's a simple operation."

"No," he said firmly.

"Does that mean you'll let me have another baby?"

"No, it does not. It means you'll be capable of having children for at least another twenty years. Anything could happen. I could get hit by a truck. You might want to have another baby by some other guy with better genes."

"No, I won't," she said. "Don't you dare get hit by a truck. What a terrible thing to say."

"Nevertheless," he said, "you are too young to do anything irreversible. I'm the one who doesn't want to risk your having my child, so this is my responsibility."

"I wish you would change your mind. There's every chance the baby would be perfectly all right. We could have a little blonde girl."

"We can adopt a little blonde girl. We are not going to discuss this. You think you can get your way with me because I've given in to you on everything lately. You can't. I made up my mind a long time ago, and I won't change it, not even for you. I told you that before we were married."

"Yes. I'm sorry." But he had also decided he would never marry, and here he was.

She finally slept, and she dreamed about Jason again. He wasn't at Stonebridge this time. He was in the house on River Valley Road. He crept down the hall to the bedroom where she and Ted slept. She was a detached observer who saw herself asleep on the bed and was unable to intervene.

Jason's hands were bloody. He stood in the doorway, tall and handsome, the beautiful man she had given herself to so willingly. "I take what is mine," he said. He put his hand inside his jacket and yanked out the small revolver he'd used at Stonebridge the night he died. Who did he kill? Nobody. The bullet had passed right through Rosalind's slim figure and into the wall. Rosalind was already dead.

"I take what is mine." He strode toward the bed and stood over the two still, sleeping figures. Rynna felt intense emotion for the man on the bed. Not fear of what

Jason would do, but a fierce love that was painful to bear. Ted, her husband, her beloved.

Jason put the revolver to Ted's head.

I take what is mine.

Jason, leave us alone. You have no business here.

I take what is mine.

He pulled the trigger.

She didn't scream. She sat up in bed, bathed in sweat but chilled right through. *God, oh, God, I can't bear this.*

Ted didn't stir, didn't wake, but she could hear his slow, even breathing. She stumbled out of bed and ran into the bathroom to be sick. This couldn't go on. She would have to ask Dr. Moran what to do, ask for a referral. After three months, the nightmares should be getting better, not worse. She must be going crazy, slowly but surely losing her mind.

She washed her face and returned to the bedroom. Everything was normal, dark and quiet. The nightmare was over. Ted was still asleep. He didn't move. She wouldn't yield to this terror. She wouldn't wake him to make sure he was all right. He was…he *was* breathing? She had heard…?

"Ted!" she said sharply. He didn't stir. "Ted!"

He came awake all at once and sat up, wincing with the pain of abrupt motion. He hesitated, unsure whether she wanted him to touch her, and then she was in his arms, and her tears were on his face.

"I'm sorry," she said. "I didn't want to wake you. I'm sorry."

"It's all right. Jesus, Rynna, you're like ice." He gathered the blankets around her shoulders. "Did you have another dream?"

"He killed you," she said.

"Jason?"

"He killed you."

He held her and rocked her as if she were a child he could lull to sleep.

"This won't stop by itself, will it?" she asked. "We'll have to do something."

"Yes. Are you warmer now? Would you like something, a cup of warm milk?"

"No, I couldn't. Just hold me."

After a while, calmer, she lay down again and closed her eyes. Ted was holding her, and she forced herself to breathe calmly, to feign sleep. When she was sure he had fallen asleep himself, she opened her eyes again.

Someone or something waited in the darkness near the door.

But the mysterious presence wasn't Jason, couldn't be Jason. He had no business here.

I take what is mine.

He was Robert's biological father.

Chapter Nine

Everything looked different in the morning. It always did. Rynna slept later than usual and didn't wake until the baby stirred. When she opened her eyes, Ted was sitting on the edge of the bed swallowing a pill without water as he often did. She laid her hand on his arm and asked, "Is that stuff safe?"

"Good morning," he said. "It's only aspirin." He touched her cheek briefly, a reassuring caress. He sounded tired.

"Not that," she said. She reached beyond him and grasped the smaller bottle. "This."

"Yes, it's safe." They were both thinking of Grandmother. "An overdose could kill you," he acknowledged. "Why? Trying to figure out how to get rid of me?"

"That's not funny," she said.

"No, I suppose not. Sorry." He rose stiffly and took a few steps to the window. "It's raining again," he said.

"Ted, sit down."

"No," he said. "It helps to move." He returned to the bed. "Call Dr. Moran today, will you? He'll know somebody you can talk to."

"Yes, I will."

He took a few more steps, slowly, stiffly, holding onto the wall, and then came back and sat on the edge of the bed. She leaned against the pillows and studied the label of the small prescription bottle. A mouthful of incomprehensible syllables, terse instructions, the name he didn't care for—Theodore.

"There's about enough to do it," he said. He sounded bitter and edgy, surely because of the pain. "Jason won't do it for you." He was referring both to Grandmother's death and to her dream.

She slapped him. He didn't understand. He couldn't say such things if he did. Her fingers stung, probably more than his face.

"Well, thank you," he said. "That was very Christian of you. Should I turn the other cheek?"

She didn't answer. She didn't care. If he was going to be like this, she didn't care.

She didn't go to class. She had never missed a lecture before, but she was in no mood for geology. For the first time, he didn't kiss her before he left.

He called during the day to make sure she was all right, but they shared no real communication. He asked if she'd called Dr. Moran, which she had. He said he would try to get home early, which he never did when he held office hours. The students wasted his time. They knew it. She knew it. He didn't or pretended he didn't. Damn it, she did love him.

When he came home, he gave her a single white rosebud. A white flag? "I think I owe you an apology," he said.

"I'm sorry I hit you," she said at once. "At the risk of sounding like Jason, you are the only person I ever cared enough to slap."

"Good to know." A gentler irony, teasing. "Let's go out to dinner."

"You don't have to make anything up to me, Ted."

She kissed him. "I love you."

****

In bed that night, Rynna touched Ted's face where she had hit him. He didn't even have a bruise. She hadn't really hurt him, but she didn't like to think she was capable of violence against someone she loved. If she was, how was she different, except in degree, from Jason?

"Forget about it," Ted said.

"I wish I could." They talked briefly, lazily, about inconsequentials. Rynna rested her head on his shoulder, quite comfortable. These moments of intimate conversation in bed were among her favorite parts of their belonging together. She found it so easy to talk this way, to confide.

"Are you afraid to go to sleep?" he asked.

"A little." How did he know? She wasn't consciously stalling.

"Would it help to talk about it—the dream?"

She didn't think so. She was already tensing up. She inhaled deeply, but it didn't help. He didn't say anything. He waited for her to take the lead. She struggled into a sitting position. Unreasonable not to be able to simply sit up in bed and hug her knees. She wasn't exactly tired of being pregnant, but it could be inconvenient.

Ted said, "I didn't mean to upset you. Please lie down."

"No. No, I'm all right."

He rubbed her back. "Does this help?"

"Yes. Thank you, sweetie." He didn't stop, and he said nothing, but she could tell he didn't like the endearment. Why did he mind? She wasn't like Fran Archer, calling everyone "honey," rather than

107

remembering their names. It wasn't a name for him, but for her most tender feelings for him.

"How did he do it?" he asked. "Jason?"

Did she want to talk about it? To make light of dreams was to rob them of their power. If she could downplay it, she would gain a small victory. She lifted her hand, index finger pointed, thumb cocked, in a child's approximation of a gun. She held it to his head and immediately swayed and shuddered. "Bang," she said hollowly and put her hands to her face. Ted didn't understand. She couldn't change the dream into something else, into mere words.

He touched her arm gently and tugged her hands away from her face. "Rynna, I'm sorry. Lie down. Please."

She didn't comply right away, but after a moment she did lie next to him. He switched off the lamp and drew her into his arms. She was safe here, or she wouldn't be safe anywhere. Her breath caught, but she shed no tears. This was her haven. "I wish we could make love tonight," she said.

"I know," he said. He kissed her. "Don't think about it." His philosophy in a nutshell—Don't think about what you can't have.

She wasn't made that way. She caressed his face, wondering if she could tempt him, persuade him.

"I know," he said and kissed her again. Definitely final, that kiss. He stroked her hair. "It's not so long. Think of Robert."

Yes. Think of Robert. They had waited in harder circumstances. Jason might invade her dreams, but at least he no longer possessed her.

She fell asleep in Ted's arms and didn't dream

again.

****

Rynna strode down the hall to the geology lab ahead of Ted, who had stopped at his office. As she approached the door, a female voice said scornfully, with the casual cruelty of the young, "But he couldn't have, Mike. He's a cripple."

"He was questioned by the police."

"Which doesn't mean—" As Rynna entered, the young woman fell silent. At least some of them now knew she was Ted's wife. They glanced at her nervously, unsure whether she had heard. She walked past them, her head high. The hell with them, all of them.

They resumed their conversation in lowered voices. She couldn't tell whether they had changed the subject.

Another student came in, a short, plump, dark-haired girl, who had talked with Rynna before. She was friendly enough and serious about her studies. She was twenty but appeared younger because of her size and the braces on her teeth. "Hi," she said as she slid into the seat across from Rynna. "I didn't see you in the lecture."

"No, I wasn't feeling well." She didn't feel well now.

"I thought maybe you'd had your baby," the girl admitted, blushing.

"No, not for weeks yet. I'll be able to finish the quarter."

"It must be hard to do both at once," she said.

"Yes, sometimes." Rynna smiled, grateful for the sympathy, the distraction.

"Would you like to borrow my lecture notes?"

"No, but thank you." She needn't know Rynna could access the professor's notes.

109

After class she stopped at Ted's office, where he was going over quiz grades with Elaine, and told him the gist of what she'd overheard.

"Don't tell me their names," he said. "I wouldn't like to be tempted to flunk them."

Elaine squeezed her arm and said, "Tell me. *I'll* flunk them."

****

She made an appointment with the psychiatrist Dr. Moran recommended. She told him about the dreams, about Jason's fatal fall, and how disturbed she was about the closet. He told her not to worry. She didn't tell him about Rosalind.

Ted didn't ask her about the sessions. He assumed she would tell him whatever she wanted him to know.

She didn't dream of Jason again, but she continued to sense, often when she was alone and sometimes when she was awake beside Ted in the silent darkness, that someone else was in the house, waiting.

****

The weather had finally taken a turn toward winter, and Rynna was glad to have a warm coat when she and Ted left the childbirth preparation class. As they headed to the parking lot, she was conscious of him, a little too quiet tonight, slowing the wheelchair to match her pace. She was extremely healthy and more energetic than ever, so not being able to walk quickly and easily annoyed her. He was aware of her frustration and sympathized, but to complain would've made her feel the most awful whiner. Everything she found awkward now was difficult or impossible for Ted, and if her back sometimes hurt, pain had been his constant companion longer than she'd been alive, and yet he was no less attentive or sympathetic than any of the other husbands in class.

He didn't start the car immediately, and she glanced at him inquiringly. "Ted?" He was more preoccupied than she had been.

"What? Oh." He turned the key in the ignition and let the engine idle briefly.

"You look sort of dazed," she told him.

"Do I?"

"Yes. It must be all those beautiful, sexy women."

He was amused. "Stop fishing. You're the prettiest one in class, and you know it."

"Only to you. I notice all the other men have an eye for Chrissy."

"Too thin," he said, "and too effusive."

"You're afraid of her," Rynna suggested.

He gave a short, humorless laugh. "Yes, as a matter of fact, I am. She makes me feel as if I'm in third grade and likely to flunk."

"You won't."

"I might. It's too bad they won't let anybody but husbands in the labor room. Lockwood would be great at this."

"Yes, she would, but I don't want her. I want you." She put her hand on his knee and leaned in to kiss him. "Let's go home."

****

They spent Thanksgiving with the Archers. Rynna had been afraid it might be a bad idea, but they enjoyed themselves thoroughly. Fran did most of the talking, of course, but she was so cheerful and generous and automatically raised everyone's spirits. George was beginning to pull out of his post-retirement depression, in large part by returning to a long-abandoned hobby of his youth. He had set up electric trains in the garage, and Ted showed what Rynna assumed to be a pretended interest in them. If it was, he was terrific about it. From his extensive library, he had unearthed two books on the history of railroads—how he found them was more than she could understand—and loaned them to George. George had a rapidly reviving interest in railroad history, while Ted was more interested in the technical aspects, and it gave them something more absorbing than the weather to discuss.

The university quarter ended, and Rynna passed mineralogy with a solid C+. Not bad, as Ted told her, for a French major. She was still undecided about going any further. If she were to enroll in his beloved geochemistry course, she would first have to take general geology and another quarter of chemistry, followed by petrology, which sounded perfectly deadly. She would, Elaine assured her, have more interesting things to do in the next few years.

The childbirth course ended too, and the certificate they earned was of more practical value than any amount of geology. She was like an athlete in training, and now she was ready for the main event.

Stonebridge had finally been leased, and she received the first check from Baxter. The amount was more than impressive. She wasn't financially dependent on Ted. With Grandmother's trust and the rent from Stonebridge, she could comfortably support herself and Robert.

She would've been happy to spend the entire check on Ted's Christmas present, but she couldn't find anything she thought would please him. She spent a lot of time looking at watches, but he liked the one he had, and she wasn't sure what he would think of the flashier features the new ones offered. She finally settled for the most mundane of gifts. Two shirts, which he would wear whether he liked them or not, and a sweater she couldn't resist. She had little hope the soft, comfortable pullover would replace his shabby favorite, but it was beautiful, oatmeal and powder blue. She would also give him two books, although she would be bringing coals to Newcastle. She consulted Elaine, who recommended a new title on geosynclinal theory. Rynna, who had to use the dictionary and still couldn't make any sense of the chapter headings, was willing to follow her advice. "Besides," Elaine said, "I can borrow it." The other book was a spy novel, currently on the best-seller list. Since he read almost everything, it couldn't be too far wrong.

On the night of December twenty-first, after putting the finishing touches on the Christmas decorations, Rynna went to bed early. She had done too much today and was so tired she was lightheaded, but not yet sleepy.

Ted brought a book to bed, which he almost never did. He read a few pages and then closed it and looked down at her lying beside him.

"I feel like a beached whale," she said. She found the one position, on her left side, in which she was ever comfortable in bed anymore.

Ted laid the book aside and slid down beside her. He rubbed her lower back. "Do you want another pillow?"

"No, nothing helps."

He rested his fingers on her abdomen, not as he used to, but in the practiced manner of a trained labor coach. "Relax," he said.

"I can't," she began and caught herself. She took a deep breath and consciously relaxed. "It's not so bad," she said contritely. "I shouldn't complain."

"When I see how uncomfortable you are, I'm glad I'm not responsible."

"Oh, really? You're just glad of something else to blame Jason for."

He didn't rise to the bait. "You are in a mood tonight," he said. "I do feel guilty, you know, in a general sort of way, on behalf of all the men in the world. We have most of the fun, and you have most of the consequences." He rubbed her back again, gently, expertly. "Relax," he urged.

She did manage to relax a little, but she was nowhere near sleep. She sighed and rolled onto her back again and then on her other side, facing him. "I miss making love," she said. "Not just physically. I feel a distance between us."

"Do you? I suppose it's my fault. I'm sorry." He took her face in his hands and kissed her until she had to pull away, breathless, clinging to him.

"That was lovely," she said, smiling, "but it wasn't quite what I meant."

"No? Cheered you up, didn't it?"

"Yes. I don't feel the least bit sexy anymore."

"You are to me. I always knew we would be good together."

"Did you?" She moved a little, restlessly, and for a split second she saw something in his face, a withdrawal. "There," she said, "that's what I mean. Don't be afraid. Do you think it would help if we talked about it? Maybe if you told me what happened with Clara…"

"I won't tell you horror stories three days before you're due."

"Don't think about them, then. I'm not Clara. And

even after she almost died, I bet she would have been willing to have another baby if she could have...Did your parents think of adopting another child?"

"I expect I was enough trouble."

"Speaking of which..."

"I knew this was coming," he said. He was amused.

"When can we start with the adoption agencies?"

"Don't you think you should make sure of this one first?"

"You won't give me an argument?"

"No, we agreed on this."

"You said you wouldn't hold me to anything I said while Jason was alive. I owe you the same courtesy."

"It's all right, Rynna. I want you to have your children."

"*My* children?"

"You know what I mean. The children you always wanted. I won't pretend I've always wanted them, but it doesn't mean I'm unwilling now. I just want to get this over with first."

"Yes," she said. More relaxed, she was finally beginning to be sleepy. "Maybe I'll just have twins," she murmured.

"Don't you dare," he said and turned off the light.

Chapter Ten

Rynna woke earlier than she would've liked from a confused dream of stress and conflict. She was having a contraction, a tightening in her belly, not too strong. She grabbed her watch without disturbing Ted and half-dozed until the next one. Eighteen minutes. Probably false. In any case she was awake now. She got out of bed and went into the bathroom. Her instinct was to wait, to proceed cautiously, above all not to wake Ted. Eleven minutes. Annoying not to be sure, but Chrissy had said false labor was normal.

"Rynna?" Ted was at the bathroom door, trying the knob. She had locked it automatically.

"I'm all right," she called.

He was silent for a moment before he tried the door again. "Rynna?"

She opened the door. "I'm having contractions, but I think it's false labor."

"Jesus," he said. "Are you sure?"

"No. I'm going to walk around and see what happens."

He didn't want to let her pass. "No, wait," he said. He was mentally reviewing what he had learned.

"Ted! Let me by."

"Yes," he said. "All right. Walk around a little. I'll get dressed."

"Don't rush," she told him. "And don't worry."

She went to the kitchen and put the coffee on and paced back and forth through the living room. The pine-fragrant Christmas tree was decorated with silver and gold ornaments, the stockings hung from the mantel, and everything was ready. If she had the baby today, she might be home, sitting here with Robert in her arms, on Christmas morning.

Ted came in, his shirt half buttoned, his hair ruffled. "Well?"

"I don't know yet." She shook her head. "I told you not to hurry. What would Chrissy say?"

He went back to shave, comb his hair, and button his shirt. When he returned, Rynna was in the kitchen poaching eggs and buttering toast. "False labor," she said "Sorry."

She *was* sorry, a little, but he let out a long breath, and his shoulders relaxed.

The rest of the day and the one following were a little tense. He tried not to watch her every minute, but it was hard, and he began to get on her nerves. She *would* have the baby during Christmas break, with him underfoot all the time. He took her out when she was restless, but it didn't help much.

She began to have contractions again on Christmas Eve, which was her official due date, but they were both cooler about it and soon determined it was false labor.

As soon as Ted was awake on Christmas morning, Rynna said, "I'm still here. Merry Christmas." While they enjoyed a special breakfast, complete with the cinnamon coffee cake she had loved as a child, she asked, "What did you do last Christmas?"

"Not much," he said. "Don't tell me what you did."

"We were at Ian and Janet's. Christmas is always

more fun with kids."

"Well, next year," he said.

After breakfast, they opened the brightly wrapped packages. "One of yours isn't here," he warned. "I'll show you later."

He opened his gifts slowly, intently. He was pleased, especially with the books, but she wished she'd given him something more, something special. "You're difficult to shop for," she told him. "You don't want anything."

"I have everything I want," he agreed.

He gave her an exquisitely frilly peignoir for the hospital and after. It wasn't practical, but it was lovely and feminine. The fabric was beautiful, rose-and-cream silk, trimmed with lace and feathers. She would never have chosen it for herself, but right now, when she felt tired, awkward, and unsexed, this little luxury was exactly what she needed to lift her spirits. "You're crazy," she said and kissed him.

"Do you like it?"

She knew he could tell she did. "I would've liked to see you shopping for it," she said. She fingered the material lovingly. "You have excellent taste."

He also, inevitably, gave her a book. Not the sort of straightforward book he liked, but a lavishly illustrated first edition of children's stories like one Clara had read to him when he was a child.

He put on one of his new shirts, her own favorite in pastel blue, and the sweater. "You're very handsome," she said. "You should always wear blue, you know. It brings out your eyes."

After they cleared away the paper and ribbons, he led the way to the garage to show her the last present. He had connived with George Archer to have it delivered next door and smuggled into the garage on Christmas Eve. Yards of red ribbon were wrapped around a shiny new dryer. A perfectly good washer had been in the garage when they moved in, but no dryer, and Rynna preferred to drive to the laundry rather than use the clothesline in the back yard.

"I thought with all the baby clothes and diapers…"

Rynna kissed him. "Ted, you are wonderful, you know, but you spend too much money on me."

"That's what it's for," he said.

They went next door for Christmas dinner with the Archers, and Rynna promised to do the cooking next year. She didn't imagine she could match Fran's golden brown roast turkey and rich homemade gravy, but she'd have a year to improve her skills. "Next year there will be five of us," she said.

"Or maybe six," said Fran, who couldn't resist teasing Ted with the prediction of twins.

****

Ted was busy preparing for the new quarter. He would teach the same two courses, and Fred Sullivan had also asked him to teach a section of general geology, lecture only, in the evening. In preparation he had visited the library once, but most of the time he worked at home, and Rynna had a sense of being constantly watched, even when she was in another room.

She was alone when her labor finally started. She was washing the breakfast dishes on the morning of the twenty-sixth, and he had gone next door to give the last of the cinnamon coffee cake to the Archers. He was gone for a long time. He must have gotten involved with George's trains, or Fran was keeping him entertained.

Rynna was singing softly to herself, her hands in hot water, when she heard a sound near the front door.

"Ted?" No answer. When he didn't come in, she dried her hands on her apron and went into the hall. Nobody. Nobody she could see. The closet door was ajar. No doubt Ted had taken his jacket and not closed it. Or he closed it, and the latch didn't catch, and the door came open again. She could shut it tightly, give it a little shove. She didn't. She stood still in the hallway, and a premonitory chill lifted the hairs on the back of her neck. Somebody was waiting.

No. Silly, superstitious nonsense. Robert's mother wouldn't behave this way. She returned to the kitchen and finished washing the dishes. Ted didn't come back, and she began to dry them and put them away.

The first contraction caught her by surprise. It was stronger than she expected, a bigger, realer sensation somehow, stabbing through her abdomen and lower back. It hurt. She held on to the sink until it passed. A watched pot never boils, she thought. What was keeping Ted?

The second one was even stronger. She bit her hand to keep from crying out. This wasn't how it should be, not the way she'd imagined it. These were not the theoretical contractions of the childbirth class, but a taste of overwhelming power that could rip her apart. She might be scared after all.

No, she wouldn't. If anything bad happened, Ted would never forgive her. As soon as she consciously relaxed and controlled her breathing, the pain eased, and her confidence returned. She could do this. She was made for this.

The contractions were regular, intense, and eight

minutes apart. When Ted returned from the Archers, she was in the bedroom. For a minute she considered not telling him, keeping her secret for a while, but she was always exasperated by the same instinct in him.

He rolled into the bedroom quietly in case she was napping. "I'm in labor," she said.

He stared at her, something dark in his face, in his eyes, fighting panic worse than her own, but he soon steadied and gathered her hands in his. "How long?"

"Only a few so far. Right after you left. It'll be a long time yet, but I didn't want to keep it from you."

"No," he said. "We're in this together." He took a deep breath. "All the time we spent in Chrissy's class and now I don't have the slightest idea what to do."

"It'll come back to you," Rynna assured him. "First call Elaine. Otherwise, she'll never forgive us."

He called Elaine. She was in the middle of laundry but came as soon as she could. She was as excited as they were and not at all anxious. When Rynna's contractions were five minutes apart, she drove them to the hospital. She escorted Rynna upstairs while Ted filled out forms. The maternity wing waiting room was a men-only club and reeked of cigarette smoke, so Elaine camped out in the nearest hallway.

Ted was allowed to put on a hospital gown and join Rynna in the labor room. It was a small, harshly lit cell with two beds and a single straight chair, and the second bed was empty. Once Rynna was settled in the narrow bed, lying in the most comfortable position she could find, she felt confident again. Everything Chrissy had taught them, carefully learned but a little unreal, worked exactly as predicted. The Dick-Read method *worked*.

Ted was terrific. The nurses were in and out, but

they were busy, and he took up the slack. Without him she would have been miserably alone most of the time. He kept his hand on her abdomen during the contractions, timed them, reminded her to breathe properly, and helped her concentrate. Between contractions he rubbed her back and talked to her, encouraging her, and offered her ice chips and juice.

The first stage wasn't at all difficult. "This is the boring part," Rynna told Ted with a sigh.

"Boring is good," he said.

The only problem they encountered was with an officious nurse who objected to the presence of the wheelchair in the labor room. The other nurse, young, efficient, and red-haired, took her outside and came back alone. "Don't take it personally," she advised. "She doesn't approve of husbands at all." She smiled at Ted. "I'm Nancy Larsen. Y'all were in Chrissy Hartman's class, weren't you?"

"Yes. How did you know?"

"I heard you mention her name. She's wonderful, isn't she?"

"Wonderful. Did you—"

"Yes. I had a boy. He's four months old. Believe me, in this job you see everything, and I wouldn't let anybody talk me out of doing natural childbirth. Some of the older doctors think it's nonsense. They still prefer mothers tied down and mostly unconscious." She consulted Rynna's chart. "Dr. Zalman. Good. He's one of the easygoin' ones. He'll give you whatever you want, and if anything goes wrong, he is *fast*."

"Can I see that?" Ted asked, indicating the chart.

"No, I'm sorry, you can't. Don't worry. We won't keep anything from you. Y'all are doing great, believe me." She gave him a thumbs up and turned to Rynna. "I have a few minutes. Would you like to get up and walk around? See if we can get gravity to help us out?"

Transition was rougher. Rynna forced herself to keep absolute concentration, and barely had time between contractions to think of anything else. She had to remind Ted to guide her breathing but "Don't distract me." This was mentally the hardest work she had ever done in her life. She didn't want to be reminded that this stage wouldn't last long or told her labor was proceeding normally. She didn't want anything, except to concentrate completely on her breathing. Ted moistened her lips and wiped the sweat from her face but kept silent.

Dr. Zalman popped in, said, "Hello," in a calm, quiet voice, and consulted with Nancy. Nancy had checked her twice with Ted in the room, but Dr. Zalman asked him to leave while he examined her.

"Why?" he asked, between stubbornness and anxiety.

Rynna, annoyed by the distraction, reminded herself how terrific he had been so far. "It's all right, sweetie," she said. "Go tell Elaine how it's going."

He was equally annoyed by the endearment, but he complied.

When he came back, he said, "You were right. It's better to be in here."

"Is Elaine worried?" she asked, but before he could answer a contraction took hold. "Don't tell me right now," she said sharply. She needed to concentrate. A few minutes later, in the second stage of labor, breathing more deeply, she was able to relax between contractions. She remembered snapping at Ted but couldn't remember what she'd said. "Did I hurt your feelings?" she asked.

"When?" he asked, bewildered. "Jesus, Rynna, of course not."

When she was fully dilated and ready to push, Nancy helped her onto a gurney and prepared to wheel her into the delivery room. Ted clung to Rynna's hand. Hospital rules barred husbands from the delivery room, but having gone this far, he didn't want to let go.

Rynna squeezed his hand and said, "Give me a kiss for luck."

He did and finally released her. "Take care of her," he told Nancy gruffly.

The delivery room was bright, filled with shiny metal equipment and stark green tile, both a bit scary, and comforting in its atmosphere of professional competence. She was transferred to a rubber-sheeted table with stirrups and handles. She wasn't afraid. She was calm, resting between contractions and talking to Nancy, but she missed Ted. Without him she was not an individual, a wife and mother, but only a patient, a body, a well-oiled baby-making machine. If transition had been difficult mentally, pushing was the real physical work. They weren't kidding when they called this labor. It was hard work.

She faltered only once. When the next contraction began, she momentarily lost her concentration.

"Breathe," Nancy said.

She breathed.

"Push," said Dr. Zalman.

She pushed.

The anesthetist stood by with the gas in case she wanted it. She would've preferred to do without, but Dr. Zalman said it was better to be prepared. She was determined to try to make it all the way without any sort of anesthetic, but she didn't want to be a martyr. Nobody would be disappointed in her, not even Chrissy. She asked the anesthetist if he was bored with nothing to do. He wore a surgical mask, but she could see the smile in his eyes. "Not a bit," he said.

She did finally give him something to do. Just once, she wanted a whiff. Breathless and a little panicky, she managed to say, "Gas."

The anesthetist held the rubber-smelling mask over her face only long enough to take the edge off, and the crisis passed.

The baby was born at 9:12 p.m. She had been in labor a little more than twelve hours. The moment of birth was the best of her entire life. Nothing in her experience, not even her love for Ted, had ever transported her to such a peak of physical and emotional exaltation.

The baby took a gasping breath and began to cry lustily. Dr. Zalman laid him on Rynna's chest. He was slippery and solid, an astonishing, sweet weight on her heart. "A nice, big, healthy boy," Dr. Zalman said.

She was astounded. He was a little bit puffy, his skin almost purple, his head slightly misshapen, and he was beautiful. His hair was dark and curly. He would resemble Jason, at least in coloring, but of course she was dark too.

"He looks like you," Nancy said.

He was no longer crying, but he squinted his eyes shut against the unreasonable brightness of this new world. After a few minutes, he opened them and, although they were still unfocused, he stared right at her. *My son.*

He weighed eight pounds, three ounces. "A nice,

big, healthy boy," Dr. Zalman said again. As soon as he was sure she and Robert were both fine, he gestured to Nancy, and she went to the door and opened it. She looked up and down the hall, making it clear they were bending the rules, and then beckoned. Ted, who must have been waiting just outside, wheeled himself in, looking both apprehensive and excited.

As he approached the bed, Rynna burst into tears. Tears of joy.

"It's a boy," Dr. Zalman told Ted.

"I told you," Rynna said. "Look, Ted, isn't he beautiful?"

She wasn't sure he had even glanced at the baby. He was looking only at her, and he put his hand on her forehead and leaned in to kiss her.

"I'm really good at this," she stage-whispered, and he laughed, sounding young and a bit shaky with relief. "I wish you could have been here," she said, and he nodded. He had yet to say a word. He finally did look at Robert. She couldn't tell what he was thinking, but he leaned over and kissed the hand that cradled the baby's head. "Say something," she urged.

He shook his head, too overwhelmed to speak, but finally managed, "I love you."

She didn't think she could ever be happier than at the moment of birth, but others could have challenged it. One of the best was when Nancy handed the baby, washed and wrapped in a blanket, to Ted. He held him and simply stared, and the expression on his face was priceless.

She had given him his special Christmas gift, and only a little late. Robert Scott Demeray. *Our son.*

****

Rynna would've liked to go home with her family right away. She wanted to have Robert with her every minute, not far away in the nursery for hours at a time. After she ate—either the hospital food was delicious, or she was starving—and slept briefly, both Elaine and Dr. Moran came in to visit her. It was long past visiting hours, but Dr. Moran had hospital privileges.

They talked quietly, trying not to disturb her roommate. She shared the semiprivate room with Mariana, a shy, dark-eyed woman who had delivered a tiny but perfect little girl by Cesarean three days before.

"Have you seen the baby?" Rynna asked. Of course they had, but she wasn't interested in talking about anything else. After a few minutes of accepting their compliments and congratulations, she asked, "Where is Ted? I haven't seen him for ages."

"I sent him home to bed a few minutes ago," Dr. Moran said. "He was exhausted."

She couldn't hide her disappointment. She wanted him close. "He didn't say goodbye."

"You were asleep," Dr. Moran said. "We should leave you now. Grab all the sleep you can, while you can."

She didn't sleep much, even though she was tired. She was too excited. The nurses, not as busy on the night shift, were sympathetic, and she wandered down the hall to the nursery to chat with them and see the babies, especially her own.

"He's beautiful, all right," one of the nurses said. "I think he's the biggest one here."

The other babies were all wonderful, especially Mariana's, with her rosebud mouth and fine hair, but none of them touched her heart the way Robert did. So tiny, each of them so perfect, but Robert was special, a miracle. He was hers.

"I like your husband," the tall, freckle-faced nurse said. "That was him, wasn't it—the blond guy in the wheelchair?"

"Yes."

"He was down here earlier. He's nuts about the baby."

Yes, apparently he was.

****

The night before Rynna was released, she slept only a few hours. While she was eating breakfast, Ted arrived to take her home. He brought her flowers, clean-scented blue and white delphiniums, not because he thought she would care about them, but to express his own feelings. Sentiment satisfied, he was perfectly willing to leave them for Mariana to enjoy.

He had seen the baby again before coming to see her. "He has fingernails," he said.

"I know," she said. "When can we go home?"

"As soon as you're ready, Mother."

She gave him a longsuffering look. "Are you going to get corny on me?"

"Probably. Dr. Zalman is signing the papers." He kissed her and took both of her hands in his. "That is one beautiful baby."

"Did you see the other babies? Mariana's—"

"What other babies?" he asked, smiling. "Yes, all right, Mariana's little girl is adorable. But ours is the best." As if on cue, Nancy came in with a blanketed bundle.

They took him home to the waiting nursery on River Valley Road. A miracle had happened, and the little house was incredibly transformed. Someone had moved in, taken over. A baby was in the house.

They didn't celebrate the New Year. With a new baby in the house, the most sensible thing to do was to go to bed early and get as much sleep as possible while they could. At midnight, the quiet neighborhood erupted into horns, whistles, and firecrackers. Rynna lay in the darkness and listened, sure she would have to go in and quiet her frightened baby, but he slept through the noise. Ted did too, as far as she could tell. When he stirred, she said, "Happy New Year."

He answered her out of an irrelevant dream. "Not before Friday."

****

In the morning, she told him what he had said. He didn't remember the dream. "Do you still dream about me?" she asked.

He stopped in the middle of buttoning his shirt to stroke her hair and kiss her just in front of her ear, which he knew she liked. "More than ever," he said.

"Good dreams?"

"Yes, and when I wake up, you're still with me. That's the best part."

It was one of the sweetest things he'd ever said. "Are you happy?" she asked.

"I have everything I want," he said. "How could I not be happy?"

"Do you? Do you have everything you want?"

He ruffled her hair, not willing to be serious. "I have you," he said, "and Robert."

"It isn't fair for you to have this responsibility now, to take on what should've been Jason's obligation. Don't you mind that Jason—that the baby might look like him?"

"No, but I'm glad he can't get custody." *I take what is mine.* "The poor bastard is dead," Ted reminded her. "Let him rest, Rynna."

If only she could.

****

Fran Archer dropped in, admired the baby, and stayed to do most of the housework. Rynna, elegantly lazy in her silk peignoir, let her. She had been half afraid that Fran, with her strong personality, would take charge and try to mother Robert. She didn't. "Honey, nobody can take care of a baby like his own mother. Raised my two all by myself. George was some help, but not much. Things were different in those days, of course. Y'all have a lot more choices now than we did then, honey, believe me." She glanced at Ted, who was holding their son again. "He's crazy about that baby."

He was. He spent hours holding him, gazing at him, breathing in his fresh, newborn smell. Weren't husbands usually jealous of the attention their wives lavished on the baby?

She was barely able to get Ted to eat regular meals. He wasn't even interested in geology. Was this the same man who never wanted to have children, who didn't want to give hostages to fortune? Did he remember his first reaction to her pregnancy? He had called it a disaster and suggested she "get rid of it." So much had happened since then. Now he was Robert's father.

Chapter Eleven

On the third night after they brought Robert home, Rynna dreamed about Jason. The details blurred as soon as she was awake. She remembered only Jason's presence, like a psychic aftertaste, annoying but irrelevant. The baby was crying.

She always heard him. She slept well enough, but more lightly now. She was a mother. Ted slept deeply and didn't always hear the baby cry, but he sometimes woke up when she got out of bed.

She went into the nursery. The room was a little chilly, and she checked the thermostat before she lifted the baby out of the crib. He stopped crying almost immediately. She sat in the rocking chair to nurse him, but he wasn't hungry. She glanced at the clock. No, he wouldn't be, and he wasn't wet either. Maybe he just wanted her to hold him. Ted spoiled him. She rocked him for a few minutes, and when she rose to put him back in the crib, he didn't stir.

"Sweet baby," she whispered, covering him with the blanket. "Sweet little Rob." Ted had begun to use the nickname right away, and she found she didn't mind at all. Rob Demeray was a good name.

She was still a little cold, regardless of the thermostat. She checked the window, but the latch was tightly closed, and she couldn't feel a draft.

When she turned from the window, the mobile

Elaine had given them was revolving above the crib, swinging gently, its tiny pigs and lambs dancing as if disturbed by a current of air.

As if someone had touched it a moment before.

Gradually the motion slowed and stopped. No doubt she had bumped the crib as she left it, or stirred the air as she walked away in her large, loose sleeves and foolish feathers. A mobile was meant to move, wasn't it? This one barely swayed unless someone touched it or the window was open, but that didn't prove anything. She was half asleep.

When she was back in bed, Ted said sleepily, "Everything okay?"

"Yes. He wasn't hungry yet. It was chilly in there. I think the thermostat needs to be adjusted."

"Okay," he said. She wasn't sure he understood. He was half asleep. In a moment she was too.

Robert started to cry again. Not energetically, but fretfully. "I'll go this time," Ted said. He started to get up, and Rynna put her hand on his arm.

"Let him cry. He's all right." He hesitated, half convinced, and then made a move to get out of bed. "You don't have to pick him up every time he cries," she said. She was too tired to argue. Which was worse—to let Ted spoil him or to hassle endlessly about what was the best thing to do? Could he teach Rob his own self-discipline, or would he be overly indulgent out of his unreasonable fear of losing him?

The baby stopped crying. Ted lay back gratefully and said, "I know what you're thinking, Rynna."

"Do you?"

"Yes. No doubt you'll be a better parent than I will. Your instincts are good. But you might show a little more respect for your elders."

She had missed his joking tone. Life had been too serious lately, too earnest. Babies sometimes wrecked marriages, damaged relationships. All the changes were overwhelming. She needed this kind of reassurance that the most basic qualities of their life were still intact. "Sorry," she said, nestling. "I defer to your age and wisdom."

"You know what?" he asked. He was relaxed, on the edge of sleep.

"What?"

"Young though you are, and pushy—"

"Am I?"

"Disrespectful. Argumentative."

"Yes?"

"I am crazy about you." He kissed her. "Now go to sleep. It's the middle of the night."

Rynna slept.

****

Two days later, Ted reluctantly returned to work. He kissed her and Robert, loath to leave them but drawn to the challenge of new students. In spite of the work involved, Rynna knew she was lucky to be able to stay home with the baby.

"Don't bother with dinner," he said. "I'll pick up something on the way home."

She assumed he meant take-out, but he came home with steaks and salad makings and did the cooking himself. He broiled her steak the way she preferred it and made sure she drank all her milk. Rynna was a little amused by this solicitude.

After she nursed Robert, she held him until his alert blue eyes gradually closed, his tiny fists clenched and relaxed, and he fell asleep. He was so beautiful, so perfect, so dear to her. The moment was so lovely, peaceful and satisfying. When she glanced up, Ted was watching her, and probably had been for some time. He had tears in his eyes.

"What is it?" she asked.

He shook his head, embarrassed.

"Tell me," she insisted gently.

"I love you," he said.

****

That night, lying beside Ted in bed, Rynna reflected that this was everything she wanted her life to be. The baby, the house, Ted happily occupied with his teaching, everything as it should be—except they couldn't yet make love.

She wanted to talk about it. Ted was amused. "You're not supposed to be interested right now."

"Who says?"

"I don't know—one of those books."

"It was wrong. Or we aren't supposed to be newlyweds. Don't you feel—?"

"No," he said, not even letting her finish.

"Would you like me to—?"

"No."

"I guess you don't feel the way I do."

"Rynna," he said, his voice colored with something between embarrassment and amazement. "What are you talking about?"

"Maybe it wasn't as good for you."

"Rynna!" He touched her face. "Are you serious?"

"I just thought…"

He slid his hand under her nightgown to rest on her thigh and bent to kiss her, sweetly, leisurely, until she ached for him. Breathless, she clung to him, and her eyes stung with tears, not for what she was missing, but for what they shared now.

"It was great," he told her. "It will be again. Now shut up about it." He lay back and took her hand, intertwining their fingers in easy companionship.

She lay quietly and contemplated this man she inexplicably loved, with all she knew about him now and so much more she didn't and possibly never would. "Tell me," she said tentatively and was aware of his immediate amusement. He thought she talked too much, but apparently in some way he liked that particular failing. "Tell me about high school. Were you a good student?"

"Yes and no. Were you?"

"It was never a problem. Were you popular with the girls?"

"Are you kidding? You know what high school is like. I suppose you dated the football heroes."

"Only one," she said. "One was enough."

"I had a car," he said, remembering. "I mean I had a seriously classy car. That was a big deal when I was sixteen. Girls used to go to the movies with me just to ride in my car."

"They probably thought you were cute."

"I wasn't cute," he said. "I was a crippled rich kid with a terrific car, and their mothers thought they were safe with me."

"Were they?"

He grinned. "Not particularly."

"No?" She moved closer and rested her head on his shoulder. She had always been safe with him, one way or another. Even when their relationship was most dangerous, the risk hadn't come from him. In a casual, just-curious tone, she asked, "Have you had a lot of women?"

"Jesus, Rynna," he said, frankly annoyed. "Are we going to start this?"

"I'm sorry. I just wanted—"

"I know what you wanted. Has it never occurred to you that you might someday have reason to be glad I don't kiss and tell?"

"Only if you left me," she said.

"Or you left me."

"Oh, Ted! I won't leave you. Sometimes I wonder how I got here. Why am I in this house? What am I doing in bed with Cousin Ted? But I like it here. I'm not going anywhere."

"All right," he said, as if he were humoring a young child.

"You can still infuriate me," she told him. "I don't know why I love you. But I do, so you'd better make up your mind you're stuck with me. I'm not Sylvia."

"You certainly aren't," he said.

No, she wouldn't ask what he meant. She didn't need him to reassure her. Whatever relationship he had enjoyed with Sylvia or with any other woman, he had married her. He was with her now. She didn't care why Sylvia left. She wouldn't be so foolish.

****

Rynna would've liked to go with Ted to his evening class. The course was designed for non-majors, and she might have learned something. But Robert was too young to take along, and she wasn't ready to leave him yet. It was still strange for him to be in the next room and no longer under her heart. No wonder mothers sometimes clung and smothered. She would try not to, but for now nothing was more important than their connection.

After she had settled him for the night and he was safely asleep for at least a few hours, she returned to the nursery several times to check on him. She was as bad as Ted, reassuring herself every few minutes. Rob was strong and healthy and safe. In time they wouldn't find it so miraculous to hear his soft breathing or so frightening to step out of the room and leave him alone.

She went into the kitchen and searched through her growing file of recipes for something different for tomorrow's dinner. Maybe she would make a rich and fattening dessert. She wanted to be thin again for Ted, but nursing was such a convenient excuse to postpone dieting. Meals had been less trouble at Stonebridge, but somehow not as satisfying. She was afraid she would be the sort of cook who couldn't resist sampling everything.

The lights blinked off.

Her heart thumped, but she didn't panic. She checked out the window to see if other lights were on in the neighborhood. They were.

She flicked switches. No lights came on. Why did this have to happen the first night Ted wasn't home?

She had nothing to fear. She knew where the flashlight was, in a kitchen drawer...wasn't it? She found it after a few minutes of fumbling in the dark. Where was the fuse box? She stood still and concentrated. She wasn't going to be frightened, was she? The fuse box was...

The lights flickered on, and Robert began to wail. Relieved, Rynna switched off the flashlight and hurried into the nursery. The mobile above the crib was swinging, not gently, but as if someone had shoved it violently and the motion was only beginning to subside.

Rynna grabbed the baby and backed hastily out of the room. No. No. She would not be frightened. Everything had a logical explanation. She stepped back into the nursery and murmured softly to Robert, comforting him. The mobile's wild motion became a gentle sway. Experimentally she put a hand to the crib and shook it. She shoved it more strongly, more abruptly than any movement of Robert's could have. The mobile swayed a little more, revolved slowly, gently.

All right, but there was an explanation. Ted would figure it out, and he would check the wiring, too.

The mobile gradually slowed. She waited until the motion stopped. Robert was asleep again, breathing slowly, completely relaxed. He was so tiny, so defenseless, so little weight in her arms. Yet he was a person, someone who could grow and change and develop day by day and begin to establish his own identity even as he showed signs of taking after her, Ted…Jason.

The lights dimmed, flickered, and went out again.

I take what is mine.

The nursery was so dark without the night light and the luminous dial of the clock that the dim light of a quarter moon made a bright square of the window. The hair on the back of her neck stood on end. It was so eerily dark, and the flashlight was in the kitchen. She made herself back slowly, carefully, toward the door. She mustn't trip or bump into anything. She mustn't wake Robert. She couldn't leave him here alone.

She found the doorway into the hall and stood still to listen. She heard nothing, saw nothing. Of course not.

"Jason?" she whispered.

She heard a noise she couldn't identify, a distant bump, a light scraping sound. Her heart raced. She made her way along the dark hall, touching the wall with one hand, holding Robert closely, protecting him.

Near the kitchen, she hesitated. She wanted the flashlight but didn't want to blunder into a room of sharp corners and half-open cupboard doors with the baby in her arms. She was afraid to go near the closet next to the front door.

In a dream, not so long ago, Jason had stood in the doorway of the bedroom she shared with Ted. She couldn't go in there, either. I'm hysterical, she thought with clinical interest. She should consult the psychiatrist again, tell him *this* story.

She stood where she was, uncertain, for a few seconds before she made her way past the entryway with its creepy closet and gained the safety of the living room. She laid the baby on the sofa without disturbing his innocent sleep and made sure he was warmly covered.

The front door opened with a loud click. She jumped and stifled a scream.

"Rynna?" Ted was home.

She was so overcome with shuddering relief she couldn't think straight. She flung herself at him, arms around his neck, half in his lap, and bruised herself heedlessly against unyielding metal.

"Oh! Ouch!" She hadn't hurt him much—he was half laughing—but he struggled to his feet in self-defense, and she clung to him, her face pressed to his chest, so grateful, filled with intense relief.

"Jesus," he said, still breathless. He leaned back against the wall, holding her. "What in God's name has gotten into you? What are you doing in the dark?"

"The lights," she said shakily and stopped to draw a steadying breath. "The lights went out."

"Jesus Christ, Rynna."

Recovering her perspective, she knew he wouldn't believe she had reason to be frightened. "I'm sorry," she said, relaxing her grip. "I'll get the flashlight."

"Be careful," he said.

She retrieved the flashlight from the kitchen counter and handed it to Ted. He studied her curiously in the dim light of the hall but said nothing. He opened the closet door, and she caught her breath. Foolish. He would be so annoyed, so amused, so damned tolerant.

The fuse box was in the closet, of course, and the replacement fuses were on the top shelf. When the lights were back on and he had put away the books she'd made him drop, Ted found Rynna in the living room, where she sat on the sofa with the baby in her arms. He sat beside her, and she gave Robert to him and leaned her head on his shoulder. He gazed at the baby for a long time without saying anything and gently stroked the fine, silky, dark hair where it curled a little on his forehead.

Finally, he asked, "Are you going to tell me what that was all about?"

"I'm sorry," she said. "Did I hurt you?"

He didn't answer. He was waiting.

"How did your class go?" she asked.

"It was fine. Tell me what happened, Rynna."

"You won't believe me," she said. Her voice wasn't quite steady.

"When have I not believed you?"

"At Stonebridge—"

"Okay, but since then?" He didn't think she would lie, but sometimes he was baffled, reluctant to believe.

She told him about the mobile and her conviction that he would know the answer.

"Thanks," he said, smiling.

"I don't like being here alone at night." It wasn't only at night, either, but she didn't want to sound hysterical. "I wish you didn't have to teach this class."

"I don't have to," he said.

"Yes, you do." She straightened and took a deep breath. She wouldn't be a liability. "It was just the lights going out."

"Was it?"

"Yes, but I don't like to be here alone after dark. Maybe if I had a gun…"

"No," he said emphatically. "No guns. Anyway, a gun wouldn't protect you from what you're afraid of."

"Do you know what I'm afraid of?"

"Do you?"

She was uncertain how to answer, and then she nodded.

"Come on." He carefully transferred Robert to her arms and reached for the wheelchair. "Let's put Robert back to bed."

They went into the nursery, and Ted switched the light on. Rynna stood still, listening. He gripped the crib rail and gave it a sharp jog. The mobile swung jerkily from side to side but slowed quickly. He turned to Rynna, a question in his eyes.

She shook her head. She went to the crib, laid Robert in it, and covered him with a warm blanket. He murmured but didn't wake. She put a hand on the mobile to stop its motion and then gave it a shove, and it responded wildly. She studied Ted's expression—skepticism, concern. "You think it's my imagination, don't you?"

He was silent long enough for her to give in to the hopelessness of unnamable fears. Finally, he said, "Rosalind wasn't your imagination."

Later, in bed, Rynna nestled in his arms, grateful to know this wouldn't come between them. However he understood what was happening, he didn't consider the problem only hers. She wasn't crazy. Something was happening, not to her, but to them.

She slept reasonably well and awoke at once, as she always did, when the baby cried. She suffered a shiver of apprehension when she entered the nursery, but everything was normal, peaceful. This was a lovely room, planned and decorated to her own taste. Nothing could be wrong here. She sat in the rocker and nursed Robert and refused to let fear in.

Ted was awake when she came back to bed. "Everything okay?" he asked.

"Yes." She snuggled up to him again, and he put his arms around her.

"You're shivering."

"It's January," she reminded him. She was warm enough, and safe. She slept again and dreamed vividly of Jason, but she wasn't frightened. He was only an annoyance.

Chapter Twelve

In the morning, while he dressed, Ted said, "I'll ask Lockwood to take the geology class for a while."

"No, Ted," Rynna protested at once.

"She can handle it," he assured her.

"I know, but Mr. Sullivan asked you to do it. He's done so much for us. You can't disappoint him just because…"

He waited, watching her.

"I don't want you to give it up," she said. "I'll…" What? Her terror might seem foolish in the morning light, but she had been genuinely frightened last night.

"Do you want to come with me?" he asked. "You could sit in my office if you don't want to come to class."

"No. Rob is too young."

He nodded soberly and buttoned his shirt, the blue one she had given him for Christmas, her favorite.

She was overcome by a rush of almost physical affection for him. "This is awful for you, isn't it?" she asked. "It goes against everything you believe."

He was surprised. "Come here," he said. She sat on the bed, still in her nightgown and the elegant peignoir he'd given her, and he put his arm around her. "What do you think I believe?" he asked.

"You believe in science. Things you can see and measure and explain with logical theories."

"Yes," he said. "Science. Theories. Why do you

think this is happening?"

"I don't know. Jason…" She hesitated. His name could always come between them. "Jason wants his son."

"Is that logical?"

"Yes, of course, but…"

Ted shook his head. "I always knew you would be trouble. I just didn't know what kind."

She bristled. "It's not my fault."

"No, it isn't, although you might have saved everyone a lot of trouble by not falling for Jason in the first place."

She was on the edge of tears. "I know."

"Rynna, I'm joking." He kissed her. "It's not your fault, but nothing like this ever happened before I met you."

"Nothing like this ever happened to me until I met you, either, and Cecile and Lucy knew about Rosalind before I came to Stonebridge. You just weren't paying attention."

"To what? Ghost stories?"

"There *was* something in the music room," she said.

"Maybe that's where the answer is," he said. He was only half serious, but Rynna took the suggestion to heart. Rosalind had always been there for her and knew Jason—or at least the uncontrollable part of him he'd inherited from his father.

She hadn't forgotten the dream that began at Stonebridge, Jason walking through the front door, out of the manor—and into their lives. Only after that dream did she begin to feel as if something frightening waited near the front door of this house. Then she had dreamed about him striding into the bedroom, where he put the gun to Ted's head and said, "I take what is mine."

He couldn't take anything unless she gave it to him. He was dead. She would protect what was hers. She would ask Rosalind to help her.

That afternoon she wrote a letter to the tenants at Stonebridge to enquire when it might be convenient for her to visit. The house still belonged to her, and Rosalind's piano was still in the music room. She would return to the place where her close connection with the Demeray family began, where she fell in love with two men and one of them died. Stonebridge had witnessed the end of her marriage to Jason, but not the end of her relationship with him. At Stonebridge, she had finally found her way to Ted.

She didn't tell him she had written. She was grateful he was dealing with the problem at all.

He held Robert for a long time that evening in front of the fireplace, and she couldn't tell what he was thinking. He said only, "He does look like you." The baby's eyes were blue-gray like Pamela's, but his hair was as dark as Jason's. She couldn't change Robert's resemblance to his biological father. The important thing was to keep him from growing like Jason in other ways.

Ted helped her put him to bed, double-checked the thermostat, made sure the window was closed, and switched on the small night light. He was as reluctant as she was to leave the nursery.

They didn't talk about it. For a while Ted busied himself with his books, but she thought he was distracted. He asked her to read a paragraph he had written and watched her as she did so. "Does it make any sense?"

"It's clear enough, but I don't understand it. I'm not much help, am I?"

145

He shook his head. "I should be able to make it clear to you. You're an intelligent woman."

"I married you. That was pretty smart."

"Yes, well, in spite of that…" He tossed his pen on the coffee table. "Let's go to bed."

"All right," she said. She wasn't tired, though. She was beginning to get her natural energy back, and she was strong and healthy. When he was tired or out of sorts, she shouldn't always think first of his arthritis. He worked hard. He had worries, distractions. She did her share to add to his burdens. He had a right to be tired sometimes.

She checked on Robert before she went to bed. Everything was in order, but she was uneasy. The sensation was too insubstantial to bother Ted with, especially tonight.

When she returned to the bedroom, he was already in bed. Rynna slowly undressed and drew the pins out of her hair. She could sense Ted watching her. The feeling was different than what she had experienced with Jason. She had been briefly, foolishly, infatuated with him and had derived considerable sensual pleasure from his intent, possessive gaze. This was something different, something that could never lead to the shuddering torment of those last weeks with Jason. She met Ted's gaze. Without moving or changing expression, he said, "You're beautiful."

She sat on the edge of the bed to give him a kiss. "Thank you, sweetie," she said, remembering too late his objection to the endearment. He didn't like it, but he didn't say anything and pulled her down beside him. Holding her with one arm, he switched off the lamp. He didn't give her a clue, so she had to ask, "What are you thinking?"

With uncharacteristic promptness, he said, "However long this lasts, it was worth it."

"Oh, Ted!" She was both moved and exasperated. "Just because I was an idiot about Jason doesn't mean I have to go on being one. I've learned a thing or two this last year. I know the difference."

"I know you do," he said. "I didn't mean—"

"I know what you meant. I want you to know I mean it too. Everything I went through to get to this point I would do again for the same result. Everything." She was thinking of the awful, unbelievable moment when Jason first struck her, the forever shattering of her idyllic happiness.

"Rynna?" She had gone rigid, remembering. She relaxed gratefully in Ted's arms, but he knew what she had been thinking. "If you hadn't married him," he said, "you probably would've left Stonebridge and never come back." She could tell it wasn't the first time he had told himself that. "We beat the odds before," he said. "We can do it again." Whatever was happening in this house was nothing to what they had been through together at Stonebridge.

****

Rynna dreamed about Jason again. He strode into the nursery where Robert slept and stood a few feet away but made no move in his direction. Did he still doubt the child was his? Could he see the resemblance? Or did he see the likeness to her that Ted saw, and eyes the color of slate? The night he died he had said, "I suppose the child is his."

And she had said, "I wish it were." She wished so even more now. She wished Jason had never come into their lives. She wished Alex had killed him when he was born.

Jason spun around and stared at her. She stood in the doorway, frozen, helpless. She couldn't run or enter to come between him and Robert. Whatever he wanted to do, he would do. "I take what is mine," he said. Yes, he did. He took more than was his. He had wanted more of her than she could give.

Rynna lifted her chin. She couldn't run, but she could speak. "He's not yours," she said.

Jason scowled and advanced on her, away from the precious life in the crib. He grew taller and swelled with rage as he approached, reeking of death.

He was going to kill her.

She screamed.

Every light in the house went out. Even the moonlight in the window was extinguished. She was in a terrible blackness, filled with screaming terror.

She woke gasping, bathed in sweat, lying in a more friendly darkness, with Ted asleep beside her. The moon wasn't up, but a faint light glowed in the window. Rain pattered on the awning.

The baby was crying.

Ted stirred but didn't wake. Her heart still pounding from the dream terror, Rynna struggled out of bed and rushed into the nursery. Everything was all right, usual, safe. The rain made a soft, friendly sound against the window. Robert was safe. He was only hungry.

Nevertheless, every hair on the back of her neck stood up. Jason wasn't there, but maybe he had been.

She lifted the baby out of the crib, and he quieted at once. She couldn't sit in the nursery, not tonight, so after a moment's hesitation, she carried him into the bedroom.

It was darker than the nursery, and she moved slowly, cautiously. Ted didn't move or speak, but he was awake. No comfortable rocking chair waited there, only the backless stool in front of the dressing table, but she had a better idea.

She checked to make sure the brake was on and eased herself into the wheelchair. Why hadn't she tried it before? The seat cushion was more comfortable than it looked.

"What are you doing?" Ted asked.

"I didn't want to stay in the nursery," she said. She didn't elaborate. If he couldn't understand, more words wouldn't help.

He sat up. "Come to bed," he said. "You'll be warmer."

She shook her head. "This is fine." Robert was certainly happy enough. She most often nursed him in the rocking chair, but if he missed the gentle motion he was accustomed to, he didn't complain.

She couldn't see Ted's expression. He asked, "Is it cold in there?"

"No, it's fine, but—"

"You don't have to explain." He might prefer not to know.

"I had a dream," she said.

"Jason." He wasn't so much resigned as unsurprised.

"He was in the nursery. I told him Rob wasn't his."

Ted made a sound of surprise or pain, a sharp intake of breath. "Was that wise?"

"It was a dream, Ted. I didn't decide what to tell him."

"I suppose not," he said, "but people do. I mean they

can learn to—face the problem and dream the solution. It's called lucid dreaming."

"Is there anything you don't know?" she asked.

"A great many things, I'm afraid. I don't know how to help you with this. I don't know where to start."

"You'll think of something," she said. "You always do." Her eyes stung with tears. He couldn't know how much she appreciated him even wanting to help.

When she finished nursing Robert, he asked, "Do you want me to take him back?"

"No." She did, but she didn't want to admit her reluctance. She wanted to be as brave as he believed she was. She was also afraid he couldn't manage and didn't want him to think she doubted him. He could drop the side of the crib and put Robert to bed without getting out of the wheelchair, but...

"Rynna," he said in a faintly reproachful tone.

She flushed. Did he know everything she thought? "I can do it," she said. She started to get up.

"No, stay where you are," he said. He got out of bed, moving stiffly—more than usual? She wasn't sure. He grabbed the handgrips. "Release the brake."

"No, Ted," she protested.

"What are you afraid of?" he asked.

Rynna gave in. She hoped he wasn't showing off. He pushed her into the nursery, slowly, but without a hitch.

Nothing had changed. The room was exactly as it had always been. The rain still pattered against the window. Whatever had changed was within her. She wasn't scared now. Ted was with her. Was everything she'd experienced only in her imagination, after all?

She rose from the wheelchair and put Robert back

in the crib, covered him with the warm blanket, and smoothed his fine, dark hair. She couldn't let anything happen to him, ever. Ted reclaimed the wheelchair and watched her. He looked much the way she felt. "Shall I push you back to the bedroom?" she asked.

"No," he said. "Go back to bed. I'll be in in a minute."

"What are you going to do?"

"Nothing. Go ahead."

Reluctantly she went. She got back into bed, shivering more from apprehension than the winter night. Ted would have wanted her to try to sleep, but she couldn't. She lay wide-eyed and waited in the darkness.

When he came to bed, he said nothing, but gathered her in his arms. Only then, warm and safe, did she sleep. She didn't dream.

****

In the morning Rynna woke first, more rested than she had been in some time. Ted was asleep, so still she could barely tell he was breathing. She propped herself on one elbow and watched him sleep. She was overcome with feeling for him, both emotional and physical. As with Robert, she couldn't bear to think anything might happen to him.

He woke up, his eyes opening to the first sight of her and to something else. "Good morning."

"Hi," she said and bent to give him a kiss, although it didn't begin to express her feelings for him.

"That was nice," he said. "What's up?"

"Nothing. I love you."

He took her words more seriously than she expected. "Do you? Still?"

"Yes. More than ever. Don't you believe me?"

151

"Yes, I do," he said gratefully and caught his breath with a sound that was only half laughter. "It's amazing."

"Ted…" Questioning him was so often a waste of time. She sought the answer in his eyes instead. "Are you in pain?" she asked.

"A little," he admitted. "Don't worry."

She remembered him walking into the nursery last night, but she didn't say anything. "Can I get you a pill?"

"No, I'm okay." He made no effort to get up, which was unusual.

She kissed him again, and nothing was lacking in his response. "Do you remember the first time you kissed me?"

"Yes. I shouldn't have."

"Maybe not, but I'm glad you did."

He touched her face, brushed her hair back, traced the outline of her jaw, and rested his fingers briefly on her lips. "More," he said, and they kissed again, not casually, but with a kind of confidence they had never enjoyed in the beginning. The difference was that they belonged together, finally.

Ted ran a hand through his hair. "What time is it?"

She glanced beyond him at the clock. "Time to get up, I'm afraid." The baby started to cry. Rynna laughed. "Like clockwork." She got up, but she didn't hurry. She pretended to be intent on pinning her hair back from her face and watched in the mirror while Ted got out of bed. He was stiff, every movement painful, and it wasn't only his knees.

"Jesus," he said.

"Shall I call Dr. Moran?"

"No, of course not." He picked up the smallest bottle on the bedside table but didn't open it. He couldn't resist a rueful smile. "Rynna, go feed the baby."

She hesitated. He had lived with this for a long time. He would know what was serious and what wasn't. She rose and went to the nursery.

When she returned, Ted was shaved and dressed, except for his shoes. Tying the laces might be difficult, and she knelt swiftly to do it for him. When she was finished, she glanced up.

"Thanks," he said.

"My pleasure." She studied his face. He looked as he always did. Maybe the pill had begun to work. "I wish…" she began impulsively.

"What?"

"I wish we could stay in bed all day."

He grinned. "And do what?"

"Listen to the rain. Talk. Make love."

"One of these days we will," he promised.

****

That afternoon Rynna took Robert out for the first time, pushing the baby carriage to the end of the street and back. The journey was a momentous one, fraught with danger. She was happy going out and happy to be back.

Ted was about a half hour later than usual getting home. At first, he was evasive, and then he said he'd had a meeting with Fred Sullivan.

Rynna didn't believe him, and she was shocked. "Ted," she protested, "You can't lie." She meant both that deceit would be disastrous to their relationship and that he wasn't any good at it. Evasion was more his style. He could usually get away with it, so why try an outright lie?

He flushed. Guilty.

"Tell me the truth. Are you having an affair with Elaine?"

He laughed. "You know I'm not."

"I'll tell her you laughed. She happens to be a very attractive woman."

"Yes, I'm sure she is, but I doubt she'd have me, and I happen to be in love with you."

"Tell me where you were, then. I trust you, but—"

"Sergeant Chandler came to see me," he said.

Rynna couldn't respond. She hadn't expected that.

"If the truth upsets you," Ted said, "I'd rather lie."

"You don't have the right to decide that."

"I know. But now you'll worry, won't you? And there's no need."

She didn't believe that either. Exasperated, she asked, "Doesn't he have better things to do?"

"Apparently not."

Months had passed since Jason's death. The police couldn't find anything new, any unsuspected eyewitnesses or sinister clues. The story was over. Why couldn't it just *be* over? "He's wasting his time," she said. "We didn't murder Jason."

"No," Ted agreed. "We didn't."

So why did she feel guilty? Sgt. Chandler believed they were guilty.

Did Jason?

Chapter Thirteen

The next time Ted taught his night class, Rynna and Robert spent the evening next door with Fran and George. Rynna enjoyed the visit and didn't admit she was too chicken to be in her own house without Ted there to protect her from Jason. Jason was dead.

That night Robert cried for a long time, and Rynna had a tough time getting him to sleep. She told herself he was overstimulated by all the attention from Fran and George or the change from their usual quiet at-home routine, but she wasn't convinced. Babies were sturdy, adaptable creatures, and Robert had so far been consistently even-tempered. He had no fever, and he didn't seem to be ill. This was nothing out of the ordinary, she assured herself. They had been lucky so far, but the baby books said spells of colicky crying were commonplace.

Ted was worried and tried not to let her know he was. She pretended not to notice. As soon as Robert was quiet, she was grateful to go to bed. She fell asleep at once.

She dreamed she was in the Archers' house, sitting in the kitchen with the baby peacefully asleep in her arms. Fran talked a blue streak while she mixed a bowl of cookie batter. Every detail of the kitchen was sharp and vivid, exactly like the reality of a few hours ago— the warm, well-lit room, Fran's easy laughter, George's half-grudging comments.

"Well, honey, isn't that just the way life is?" Fran said, shaking her head.

"If you say so," Rynna said, smiling. She glanced at Robert, the sweet curve of his cheek, those tiny, curled fingers, and back at Fran. Beyond Fran, something flickered in the uncurtained window. Rynna frowned. At first, she could make nothing out, but gradually the image became clear.

Jason's face, a face with bold, dark eyes, unsmiling, watching her.

The baby stirred in her arms and opened his eyes.

Jason beckoned.

Robert screamed.

Rynna woke in terror, and the baby was really crying. The dream had disoriented her, and she needed a few seconds to realize she was in her own bed and the baby was in the next room.

Ted was sitting on the edge of the bed. "I'll go," he said.

"No," she said. "It's all right." Her teeth were chattering, but she got up, pulled on her robe, and hurried into the nursery.

Robert was not wet, not hungry, not interested in being held, rocked, or comforted. He simply screamed, as if in rage. He had no fever, nothing pinching or binding, no pins sticking into him. He cried and cried and cried, a shrill. grating sound.

Ted came in, pale and tired, his mouth a grim line, his hair tousled. "Maybe we should call Phil Moran," he said.

"He wouldn't appreciate being awakened in the middle of the night any more than you do," she pointed out. She was unreasonably annoyed with him. The baby's crying must be getting on his nerves as well as hers. She was worried too, but determined to be sensible about this, not to blow the problem out of proportion.

"Maybe…"

"He's all right. I'm not going to call Dr. Moran. He would only say—"

"Okay, okay." He might not have been as annoyed as he sounded. She couldn't tell because they had to shout to be heard.

"Please go back to bed," she said. She paced back and forth and bounced Robert a little. He didn't like the motion. He didn't like anything she did.

"Isn't there something—?"

"No. I've tried everything. Please go back to bed. Try to get some sleep. You have class tomorrow."

He didn't leave, and she walked toward the window with slow, bouncing steps. "Shh," she murmured. "Hush, baby." Behind her Ted jerked the wheelchair around and went out. She didn't think he would sleep. Who could sleep?

After a few minutes she grew calmer. Getting frazzled and impatient wouldn't help. Her agitation would only upset Robert more. If she focused on calm, soothing thoughts, she might be able to communicate them to him. In any case, she would have to wait this out. She couldn't do anything more.

Finally, when she was half asleep with near exhaustion, his cries grew less frantic, less outraged. He allowed her to soothe and comfort him. Slowly, carefully, murmuring softly, she laid him on his side in the crib. He fussed briefly, but when she gently rubbed his back, he quieted. At last, he was still.

As she straightened and stepped back from the crib, the night light dimmed for a second, not as if the bulb were dying, but with the split-second flicker of something passing in front of it. She shook her head. She was half asleep. Imagining things.

The mobile above the crib began to sway.

She hadn't touched the railing. It wasn't losing momentum after a sharp movement.

The slow oscillation increased.

Every hair on the back of her neck stood straight up. A chill ran the length of her spine, partly terror, partly reaction to a real drop in temperature. The room was abruptly colder than a moment before.

She snatched Robert out of the crib and rushed out of the nursery. He protested but didn't begin to wail. She stopped inside the bedroom door and waited for her eyes to adjust to the deeper darkness. "Ted," she said. She was almost whimpering.

If he was asleep, he came awake immediately. He sat up, galvanized by what he heard in her voice, and switched on the lamp. "Jesus, Rynna," he said. "You look like you've seen a ghost."

Poor choice of phrase. She almost laughed. Instead, she thrust the baby into his arms and closed the door. It wasn't enough. She locked it and dragged the dressing table over in front of it, spilling brushes and lipsticks. Not enough. She tugged at the dresser, but it was too heavy for her.

"Rynna!"

"Jason," she said. "Jason—"

"Rynna, stop it." She didn't like his tone, as if he were about to get up and slap her.

"He's there," she said. "He's in there. He's in the

nursery."

Ted, the voice of reason, said flatly, "Jason is dead."

"I know. I know he is. I'm not crazy." She was almost sobbing.

"Hey," he said in a softer tone. "Come here."

He laid Robert on the bed, covered him with the quilt, and held out his arms to Rynna, who gratefully found refuge there. "He's in the nursery," she said. "I can't leave Rob in there. I can't."

"All right," he said. He held her and stroked her hair.

As soon as she could catch her breath, Rynna said, "Now you'll tell me to see the psychiatrist again."

"I'm not going to tell you anything." After a few minutes he said, "At least Rob is sleeping. I'd suggest we do the same."

"I can't—" she began.

"Shh." Ted kissed her and brushed her hair back from her face.

"I'm scared. I—"

"We'll talk about it in the morning. Take a drawer out of the dresser."

"What?"

"Do it." She did and gave it to him. He unceremoniously dumped the contents on the floor and laid a pillow in the drawer to make a temporary bed for the baby.

"Oh," said Rynna. "Thank you." She lowered the drawer to the floor on her side of the bed, farthest from the locked and barricaded door, farthest from the nursery. She settled Robert in his makeshift crib and lay down, keeping one hand on the drawer. Nobody would take him from her.

Ted switched off the lamp. "Good night."

He was asleep almost at once.

She was awake for over an hour, worn out but unable to relax.

****

They didn't talk in the morning. Rynna, exhausted, slept late. Ted made his own breakfast, gave Robert a bottle, kissed her briefly, and told her to go back to sleep. He had shoved the dressing table away from the door, but it still stood out from the wall, mute evidence of her panic. The terror of last night seemed unreal and foolish now, and yet she was convinced she hadn't imagined anything. She had no idea what he thought.

She stayed out of the nursery all day, not sure what she feared to find. She was a little nervous even being in the house alone, but she worked at being calm and sensible, lest she upset Robert. She did her housework with unusual energy, made a special dinner of scallops with lemon herb sauce, and baked cookies. It was a lot of work, along with caring for the baby, but she needed to be busy, to keep occupied.

Nothing was said at dinner. Ted did notice the extra effort she had made but didn't speculate on her motives. He told her about his day and said nothing to suggest he even remembered the drama of the night before.

As she rose to clear the table, Rynna said, "You think I'm crazy, don't you?"

He gazed at her without surprise, his expression a little guarded. "Yes," he said, with a hint of a smile. "You gave up a beautiful Georgian mansion, Jason's entire estate, and your independence to live here with a boring geology professor who can't take you dancing. You *are* crazy."

She shook her head. "I gave up a drafty mausoleum,

160

a foreign car I was afraid to drive, and the joys of unwed motherhood to marry the man I love."

"Yes, you always would have the man you wanted, whether it made any sense or not."

"This time it does," she said. He couldn't get at her by teasing her about Jason. She came up behind the wheelchair and put her arms around him. "Ted…"

"This is nice," he said.

She wouldn't let him distract her. "When I first told you about Rosalind, you thought I was crazy, didn't you?"

"Yes, and you thought I was gaslighting you."

"I didn't know you yet. I didn't know what a bad liar you are, and you had no reason to credit my sanity."

"And now I do. I believe you, Rynna."

"Do you?" She bent and put her cheek against his. "I'm not talking about dreams. Something is there. Lights flicker. The mobile moves. Those things are real."

"All right," he said. "Sit down." She sat back in her chair, and Ted took her hands in his. "What do you think causes all this?" he asked.

"Jason," she said. Hadn't he been listening?

"Yes, all right, Jason. But that's the name you give to it, because of the dreams you've had. But what is it? What makes lights blink and objects move?"

"Energy. Some kind of energy."

"Okay, let's assume it's some kind of energy. Psychic energy, if such a thing exists. Where does it come from?"

"I don't know, Ted."

"From you? They say poltergeist activity is caused by excess kinetic energy from certain people."

"Yes, poltergeists," she said. "Pans thrown out of

cupboards and things like that, and usually with teenagers. This isn't a poltergeist."

"I didn't say it was. You see things. I don't."

"You saw the lights out when you came home."

"That was a blown fuse."

"You saw Rosalind."

He evaded her intent gaze. He didn't like to remember that. "I'm not talking about Rosalind."

"It's not coming from me. I know it isn't. Rosalind was there before I was. If Jason is here, it's not my fault. I don't want him here."

"I'm not saying it's your fault."

"Robert feels something too," she said. "I won't leave him in the nursery. Jason frightens him."

He stared at her helplessly. "Jason is dead," he said, as if repetition would make it true.

"You don't understand," she said, despairing.

"No, I don't. All right, all right. You think Jason is doing this. What does he want?"

"His son."

"Okay, but he can't have him, and he can't hurt him. Robert isn't afraid of ghosts. He's upset because you are. If this is some form of energy we don't understand yet, it isn't a powerful force. There isn't much of it, barely enough to make a little mischief, scare you a little. It can't hurt Rob."

"Rosalind killed Jason," she reminded him.

"No, she didn't. She never laid a hand on him."

"She played the piano."

"That's not a lot of energy either. Is it?"

"No." He was trying to reassure her, to convince her they were in no danger, but he only succeeded in making her feel more alone. If he thought he could talk her into leaving her baby alone in the damned nursery, he was badly mistaken. "Ted, how much energy would it take to kill a baby?"

"Nobody wants to kill him."

"Jason wants his son. He wants to possess him. How much energy would it take to smother a baby? If he can interfere with the electricity, couldn't he—?"

"Don't go off the deep end here."

"I'm not. You don't know what could happen." She took a deep breath. As wrong as it was to use his own fears against him, she couldn't resist. "What if that's what crib death is?"

"Jesus, Rynna." She had gone too far.

"I don't care," she cried. "I'm not crazy. I won't risk my son's life. We have to *do* something."

"What? What do you want to do? Are you going to barricade the bedroom door every night?"

"No." She wanted to, though.

"What, then? We've barely settled in here. Do you want to move again?"

"No. If he followed us here, he could follow us again."

"Jesus," said Ted. He let go of her hands and backed the wheelchair away from the table. He was exasperated, and Rynna was afraid he would leave the room, as he used to when they argued at Stonebridge. The arguments were always about the same thing.

Jason. Even now Jason could divide them. He would never let go.

"You don't understand," she said.

"Don't say that. I'm trying to understand. I don't know what to do. Give me a chance to think about this. Jesus!"

Rynna went to him and kissed him. "Whatever happens," she said, "don't let this come between us. That's the most important thing."

"Jason would like that, wouldn't he? To break us up?"

They did the dishes and didn't talk about it again. The subject was still on Rynna's mind, and she knew Ted was thinking about it too but didn't question him. He was right. He needed time. She saw things, sensed things, and she knew what was happening. To Ted, these occurrences were still a mystery, an unknown. He still thought she might be imagining most of it.

She locked the bedroom door but didn't put up a barricade. Robert slept again in the drawer bed on the floor. The situation had its advantages. When he cried in the night, she was nearby. The arrangement couldn't be permanent, but for now it would do.

Chapter Fourteen

A few days later, Ted and Rynna left Robert with Fran Archer for the first time. Elaine agreed to handle the mineralogy lab so they could keep an appointment with an adoption agency. At first Rynna had wanted to take Robert. She hadn't yet been truly separated from him. He was always where she could walk down the hall and reassure herself that he was all right.

A lot of people were seated in the large waiting room, as subdued as the beige décor, people who had tried and hoped for years to achieve what she had accomplished effortlessly. Even though she was sure they were doing the right thing, Rynna felt guilty.

When it was their turn, they were escorted into a small room and asked a lot of questions, a lot more than she expected. To establish their eligibility as parents, they gave the agency permission to examine all their records. Nothing was wrong with their finances, anyway, or their educational backgrounds, and Dr. Moran would attest to their general good health. Now she wished she hadn't seen the psychiatrist, especially as the sessions had done her little good. He had told her not to worry. He might tell the agency the same thing—that her reactions weren't unusual. She hoped they wouldn't talk to Ian Wyatt.

Ted answered every question candidly and completely. He told the caseworker things he had never told her. He was doing it for her, to make sure nothing would stand in the way of their chances. She had never loved him more.

In the car, he said, "Thank God that's over. Talk about the third degree."

Rynna kissed him warmly. "You were wonderful," she said.

****

After the initial interview, a caseworker made an official visit. For one day at least the nursery was warm, cheery, and freshly dusted. Rynna showed the caseworker the house with pardonable pride in what she had accomplished She didn't hesitate to go into the nursery. It was a lovely room.

Where, asked the caseworker, would the new child sleep?

Rynna was elated. Something might actually come of all these questions. The room Ted now used as a study could be converted into a bedroom, she explained, although they might buy a bigger house later.

She picked up Robert, who was fussing a little, and carried him with her to see the caseworker to the door. He was proof of her qualifications as a parent. He was clean, well-fed, healthy, happy, and alert. She was justifiably proud of him. The caseworker didn't need to know he'd slept in a drawer for the last few nights or that his mother believed in ghosts.

Afterward, she returned to the nursery. As she passed through the door, the mobile began to swing. Rynna backed out and slammed the door as hard as she could.

Robert, startled, wailed.

"God damn you, Jason," she said aloud. He knew

exactly what he was doing. He was defying her, baiting her. She had set about the business of adopting a baby, hoping to welcome another child into this house, as if everything were as it should be. Very well, he would remind her of his claim on the child she had now. He would take what was his.

"No, you won't," she said. "You won't."

****

Rynna would have been less nervous about leaving the baby with Fran the second time, but in the end, she decided to take him with her to Stonebridge. She would take him back where he had been conceived in love—or something like it—and appeal to Rosalind to intercede on his behalf.

She was surprised to feel apprehensive when she approached the house. She sat in the car for a while, reminding herself how elegant the Georgian architecture was. She had been so happy here—and so unhappy.

Lucy opened the door. "Mrs. Wyatt!"

"It's Demeray now," Rynna reminded her.

"Oh, yes."

"And this is Robert," she added, presenting the baby for Lucy's approval.

"He looks like you," she said, but the words were mere politeness.

"Ted thinks so too."

For some reason, Lucy was embarrassed—by the mention of Ted's name? She led the way into the house, explaining that the tenants were gone for the day and Rynna was to feel free to take all the time she wanted.

Rynna stopped in the entry to admire the fine woodwork once more. Lucy hovered, a little anxious. "Shall I take the baby for you?"

"No, thank you. I won't stay long, but I want to spend a little time in the music room."

Lucy nodded, started to leave, and then hesitated in the doorway.

"What is it, Lucy?"

"Oh, Mrs. Demeray, I'm so sorry about what happened. I feel like it was my fault."

"No, of course it wasn't."

"I knew something might happen. He wanted me to stay out of the way. I knew—I knew he hurt you before. I wish I—"

"It's all right," Rynna said. "You didn't do anything wrong." She refused to blame herself or Ted, much less Lucy. The ultimate responsibility was Jason's.

She went into the music room. The dark wood and deep pink wallpaper were unchanged, but the familiar warmth and charm were diminished. A bigger shock was that Rosalind's portrait was gone. She might've known it would be, with none of the family living in the house. The tenants had probably stored it away in the attic, face to the wall. It was only a picture.

She sat on the mahogany piano bench with Robert cradled in her arms and closed her eyes. The room was cool and clean and smelled of furniture polish and cut flowers. She waited. Nothing happened. Rosalind wasn't here. Useless to appeal to her on behalf of her grandchild. She should be glad to know Rosalind was at rest, but she only felt bereft.

****

Ted embarked on a more scientific approach to the problem. He brought home several dozen books from the university library, the public library, and two different bookstores.

"We don't have room for any more books," Rynna told him.

"We can put them in the nursery," he said. The nursery remained unused.

The books were about psychic phenomena. Most of them were scientific studies, with a sprinkling of folklore. Ted did what he always did with more concrete subjects. He immersed himself in the available literature, scribbled copious notes, and acquired the jargon effortlessly. He concentrated on one aspect of the subject—how to get rid of a ghost. He took it seriously as a field of study even if he didn't expect any of the techniques to work.

Rynna didn't know what to make of all this. She changed Robert's diaper and buttoned him into the tiny green overalls Fran had given him, while Ted explained how to exorcise an unredeemed soul. She didn't put any stock in these theories, although if unredeemed souls existed, Jason would certainly qualify.

"You sound like a ghost hunter," she said, teasing.

"Ed Warren or Harry Price?" he asked, citing the paranormal investigators who had authored some of the books.

"Neither one. You're much better looking than either of them," she said.

"Very funny."

"Well, you are."

Robert grinned and cooed.

"What's so funny, Rob Demeray? Don't you think your daddy is awfully handsome?"

They heard a clattering noise, not loud, but startling, from the direction of the nursery. Ted and Rynna exchanged a glance of mystified amusement. "I will if you will," he said, and they went together to investigate.

The mobile, which Ted had securely anchored to the headboard, was in a heap in the crib, right where the baby would have been lying. Ted picked it up and examined the bracket. "That could've been dangerous," he said.

"I told you it wasn't safe," she said. He was taking this too calmly. Did he think the bracket had snapped by itself?

"Yes, you did." He glanced at the crib, at the mobile in his hands, back at the crib. "Give us a break, Jason," he said abruptly. "What do you want?" No response came, of course. Nothing happened. Ted looked at Rynna and shrugged. "Do you feel anything?"

"No." She thought of something, something she would have preferred not to put into words, but it was too late.

He waited, eyebrows raised, for her to explain.

"Why did this happen right now?" she asked.

"We were talking about…" He couldn't remember.

"I was talking to Rob. I called you Daddy."

"And Jason didn't like it?"

"He wouldn't, would he? Do you remember what he said that night?"

Ted searched his memory for the exact words. "He said if the baby was his, nobody else was going to raise him."

" 'Least of all Demeray.' " She remembered with a sickening chill the dream in which Jason killed Ted. She said, "Maybe he doesn't want Rob. Maybe he just doesn't want you to have him."

He coolly considered this theory and said the last thing she expected. "Do you want a divorce?"

"No," she said, a little shaky. She didn't think it was

funny. She wasn't sure he meant it to be. Divorce wasn't a traditional method of exorcism.

If he was serious, he gave no sign. He gestured toward the mobile. "What are we going to tell Lockwood?" he asked.

****

They didn't invent a story for Elaine. Ted accepted Rynna's verdict that he wasn't a good liar and deferred to her for an explanation, and she didn't have one. Elaine glanced from one to the other, mystified, and finally Ted said, "I think we should tell her." Instead of saying anything, he handed her one of the books, the one he found most informative.

She glanced at the title and was immediately enlightened. "Oh," she said, flushed with pleasure. "You have a ghost."

Ted gave her a daunting look. "It isn't our idea of great fun," he said. "It has Rynna very upset."

Elaine raised her eyebrows at Rynna. "It?"

"He," she said. "At least I think it's…" She hesitated. She wasn't sure she wanted to say his name. Still, this was Elaine. "Jason," she said.

Elaine was suitably impressed. "What are you going to do?"

"Get rid of him," Ted said and couldn't resist adding, "Again."

Coolly matter-of-fact, she said, "But you didn't kill him, did you?"

"No, we didn't," Rynna said. She stood behind Ted's wheelchair and put her arms around him to present a united front. "It's high time he left us alone."

He didn't, of course.

Two nights later she dreamed they were all back at

Stonebridge. They were, for some vague reason, in Pamela's room, exactly as it had been when she first saw it, a girlish blue-and-white room with a handsome fireplace. Ted and Jason began to argue, not loudly, but with increasing tension. Fearful they would wake the baby, she carried Robert into the next room—a nursery much like the one on River Valley Road—and surrendered him to Lucy. She returned to Pamela's room, determined to end this incessant quarreling.

She hurried into the room, where Jason brandished a long, sharp, deadly blade. He threatened Ted with the knife, which only increased his defiance. "Stop it right now," Rynna said. She was addressing both of them equally. Ted had deliberately provoked Jason. "Jason, I won't have a weapon in my house. Get rid of it."

He hesitated and lowered the knife. He wouldn't defy her. She was mistress of Stonebridge.

Ted said something she didn't catch, not more than three words. She should have understood. It might be important.

Jason understood. He lunged quickly and buried the knife to its hilt between Ted's ribs.

Rynna screamed.

The wheelchair overturned, and Ted was lying on the floor, his glasses shattered beside him. A trail of bright, red drops followed Jason to the door, where he stood holding the dripping knife.

Somehow this was familiar. Shattered glass, drops of blood—they belonged to the one unfulfilled vision she'd had at Stonebridge.

She woke up, frightened but determined not to give in to panic. She was sure the dream contained a clue if she could only figure out the meaning. What did Ted say that provoked Jason? If she could decipher those words, she would know how to fight back.

She moved quietly so she wouldn't disturb Ted and sat on the edge of the bed. Robert was asleep, his breathing steady. She patted him lightly to reassure herself and started to get up.

A hand closed on her wrist, holding her there. She gasped, startled, and turned to chide Ted for frightening her. He didn't answer and she reached to turn on the lamp with her other hand.

He was asleep. Both of his hands were visible. She jerked her arm and the sensation of strong fingers holding her vanished. Maybe she had still been dreaming. She rubbed her wrist and whispered fiercely, "Jason, please."

Ted stirred, and she was overwhelmed with need for him. She was in his arms, half on top of him, before she could think any further.

He woke up and instinctively fended her off.

"Ted!" she said tearfully. The rejection—it was only self-preservation but felt like rejection—was too much to bear.

He was fully awake now and realized what she was feeling. He drew her to him, his face in her hair. "Sorry," he murmured. "I'm not much good to you, am I?"

"Don't say that."

"You're shivering. Did you have a nightmare?"

Bright drops of blood, shattered glass. "Yes." She didn't need to tell him about it. She remembered the hand on her wrist and shuddered, but it was part of the dream. She nestled against Ted. "You know what?" she asked.

"What?" he asked, a shade absentminded, his hand on her hair.

"I love you."

"Yeah? That's good." He was smiling—she could tell without looking. "You know what?"

"What?"

"We're going to put the stubborn bastard to rest finally."

Rynna lifted her head to study his face in the lamplight. She couldn't read his expression. "Are we?" she whispered, remembering the long, wicked knife.

"Yes," he said. "We are."

****

Ted certainly tried.

He did the simple things first. They were less trouble and appealed to his sense of order. They shouldn't need nuclear weapons to kill a gnat. The uncomplicated ceremonies that worked in folk stories were the logical place to begin.

Ted visited the Catholic church three blocks away and returned with a small vial of holy water. Rynna couldn't see why religious rituals would have any effect if Jason didn't believe in such things. What they needed was an expert, somebody who knew what he was doing. A ghost hunter, a medium, a priest. She didn't have to think through her feelings about such an undertaking, because Ted wouldn't even consider the option. Telling Elaine was bad enough. They would solve the problem themselves.

Working hard at the proper solemnity, he sprinkled holy water in the nursery and, after some hesitation, in their bedroom. Rynna asked him to use some in the hallway closet. He did as she asked without comment.

Afterward, Rynna felt nothing but a sense of anticlimax. The logical thing to do was to go about her business, firmly believing they had solved the problem.

That night she had an incredibly vivid dream about Jason. This one wasn't related to his death or the baby. She was married to him, in love with him, unable to understand why she had such a strong conviction that he intended to kill her.

"What have I done wrong, Jason?"

He shook his head. If she didn't know, so much the worse for her. She ought to know. What kind of woman was she?

When she woke up, she thought, Jason is dead. Having had feelings for him in the dream hurt. She had loved him. How could he want to kill her? He was handsome, charming, a "catch." Was she betraying Ted by remembering him in a positive light? Would Ted begrudge her the little good she could salvage from the tragedy of her first marriage?

No. He loved her. She touched his shoulder, but he didn't stir. Whatever she had felt for Jason in the dream, she felt more deeply for Ted. He would do anything for her—anything he *could* do.

The baby stirred and whimpered a little. She sat up and checked the time. He wouldn't be asleep for long. She should take him out and not disturb Ted. The nursery was safe now, wasn't it? The holy water would have done its work, and Jason was at rest. She and Robert had missed the rocking chair during these early-morning feedings. She wasn't afraid of the dark.

She carried him into the nursery and rocked gently in the rocking chair while she nursed him. The room was calm and peaceful. She had achieved an important personal victory through an ordinary routine. When he was satisfied and sweetly asleep in her arms, she got to her feet and stood next to the crib, hesitating. She had become accustomed to having him so near. Would Ted think her a coward? Given the choice, would he leave the baby here alone?

She felt a draft, half turned toward the window, and something moved, flickered, and vanished. Her heart pounded, but she stood her ground. If the window were slightly raised, the curtains would ripple in a gust of wind. For several seconds she waited, listening hard. She heard nothing. She couldn't bring herself to walk across the room and make sure the window was closed. It should've been closed.

Jason…

She took Robert back to the bedroom, but for more than an hour she didn't sleep and kept her hand on his makeshift cradle.

So much for holy water.

****

They used it again, though, with more ceremony. Ted said the Lord's Prayer. Rynna suggested the Twenty-Third Psalm—"Yea, though I walk through the valley of the shadow of death, I will fear no evil." The shadow of death, where Jason still lurked, unwilling to leave.

She continued to dream of Jason, familiar dreams, many of the same incidents recurring. She couldn't visit the nursery except in broad daylight with Ted in the house.

The day of his next night class, he came home with a frisky cocker spaniel puppy.

"Oh, Ted, it's so much trouble to have a dog in the city," she objected. "You really shouldn't—oh, he is sweet." She scratched the dog's floppy ears and nuzzled his little nose.

"If you don't want him, we can take him back," Ted said, even as he leaned over to set him on the floor.

The puppy skittered through the living room and into the kitchen. Rynna couldn't help smiling, even though she was exasperated. "You didn't say anything. What were you thinking of? I don't want a dog. Robert is too young. When he's older—"

"We can take him back," he said again. He wasn't at all disconcerted by her reaction. "I would have talked to you first, but it was an impulse. I thought maybe you wouldn't be scared tonight."

"Oh, Ted." She grabbed the puppy before he could topple the wastebasket. He squirmed in her arms and licked her face. "I don't know. He is cute, but the yard is too small, and we'll have to feed him and walk him and take him to the vet and keep him away from the baby and—oh, Ted!" She was between annoyance and surrender.

"Okay," he said. "We'll take him back. Keep him tonight, though. He won't cause total disaster in one night. He's housebroken, anyway."

"Are you sure? Where did you get him? I can't believe you did this. What's his name?"

"They were calling him Corky," he said. "You can change it if you decide to keep him. I thought you might feel less alone. If it doesn't work, you can always go next door again."

Corky squirmed, anxious to get free, and Rynna put him on the floor. He raced through the kitchen and dining room, exploring, and sniffed eagerly at her shoes and the wheelchair tires. Back and forth he raced, curious and excited.

"He'll break something," she predicted. She followed the puppy toward the bedroom, intending to intercept him before he could disturb Robert, who had just gone to sleep.

At the door of the nursery, Corky stopped short. He sniffed, whined a little, and backed away, puzzled and frightened.

The hair on the back of Rynna's neck stood up.

Ted was right behind her, and he saw the dog's reaction too. "Damn it," he said, obviously impressed. "They say animals can sense things we don't."

"*You* don't," she said, before she could think better of it. She meant that he still didn't believe as she did, still thought the problem was mostly in her mind. The little rituals he performed were for her benefit, not Jason's. The mobile had convinced him, but with time he could forget conviction and rationalize. Corky didn't need to be convinced. He simply refused to go into the nursery.

"All right," said Ted. He wasn't going to argue.

She kept Corky "just for tonight" and she did feel safer. He would surely warn her of any new danger.

****

At breakfast the next morning, they discussed the situation rationally, leaving Jason out of the equation, and concluded that, adorable as Corky was, this wasn't the best time to add a puppy to their household. Maybe when Robert was a little older. She expected Ted to be disappointed, but he wasn't. He'd followed an impulse, an idea of something he could do for her. He was always thinking of her. Rynna kissed him warmly. "Thank you, sweetie. I'm sorry."

"Nonsense," he said at once. "Next time I bring you a present, I'll be sure you'll like it."

"I do like Corky." Yes, he was a cute little creature, and he knew what was what. Prayers and holy water were of no use. The nursery wasn't safe.

That night after she had put Robert to bed in their room, they enacted another solemn ritual in the nursery. This ceremony was a little more serious, had a little more purpose. Corky's reaction had reminded Ted of the reality of all this, and he was more sincere.

They sat together in the dark, and he lit two votive candles like those burned in Catholic churches, short, stubby wax candles in brightly colored glass holders, and set them on the dresser. Again, they sprinkled holy water and together, holding hands before the flickering candles, they intoned the Lord's Prayer and the Twenty-Third Psalm. As a ritual of exorcism, it was solemn and impressive, the best yet.

Ted studied her—hoping she would sense something?

She shook her head.

They waited in silence, scarcely breathing. The prayers and holy water hadn't worked before. The candles added a touch of ambient charm, but the procedure was the same. Was there any hope?

The candles snuffed out abruptly, both at once, and the glass containers shattered with a sharp, explosive sound.

Rynna couldn't remember how she got out of the nursery. She was in the hall, so terrified she didn't know whether she was hurt or not. She was on her knees, holding onto the wheelchair, her face against Ted's chest, his arms around her.

"Jesus Christ," he said. "Are you all right?"

"I think so." She could barely breathe, but she began

to feel, under her terror, also elated. They weren't merely whistling in the dark. She stared at Ted. His hands were bloody. She thought sickeningly of the dream in which Jason had arisen from the dead at Stonebridge, blood on his hands and dripping from his head, and then she steadied. No real damage had been done, only a few minor cuts from broken glass on Ted's hands and hers. "I'll get the antiseptic," she said.

He shook his head. He was shaken, but he was elated too, as she was. "We need more than antiseptic," he said. "We're playing with fire."

That night Ted was the one who closed and locked their bedroom door.

****

After some discussion, Ted and Rynna told Elaine about the incident with the candles. They invited her to dinner and discussed the subject over spaghetti and garlic bread. She was impressed and wanted to see the trick repeated.

"This isn't a game," Ted said sternly.

"Lighten up, Demeray. I know it's serious, but it's damned exciting, isn't it?"

"In a way," Rynna admitted.

"What we need," Ted told them, "is a way to communicate with Jason. In all these books—"

"Never mind the books," Elaine said. "Try the candle trick again."

"It's dangerous," he said. "Anyway, what you want to do is convince him he's dead. Mediums do it all the time. He might not know he's dead. Or if he does, we need to find out why he's still hanging around, what will satisfy him so he'll leave us alone."

Elaine gave Rynna a mischievous smile. "Do you

believe what you're hearing?" she asked. "Professor Demeray has bought the whole bill of goods."

"Shut up," he said, but he wasn't offended. He was beyond personal feelings, for the time being at least. Something real was happening. Nothing else mattered.

"Okay, okay," Elaine said. "What do you want us to do, Professor?"

"Stop calling me that. I told you. We have to figure out how to communicate."

The phone rang.

Elaine laughed.

Ted, smiling in spite of himself, said, "That isn't what I meant," and went to answer it. When he returned, he was more subdued. "The adoption agency," he said.

"Oh," said Rynna faintly. The real world still moved on.

Elaine knew they wanted to talk alone. "Listen," she said as she rose to leave. "I'll bring my Ouija board next time, if I can find it."

When she had gone, Rynna turned tremulously to Ted.

"We have an appointment," he said and, before she could ask, "I don't know what it means."

Chapter Fifteen

Ted and Rynna's appointment wasn't with the
caseworker who'd interviewed them the first time, or the
woman who had come to the house, but a Miss
Harrington, young, slender, and dark-haired, with an air
of brisk efficiency tempered with sympathy. Her office
was tastefully appointed, with surprisingly comfortable
visitors' chairs, and as welcoming as she was.

Rynna couldn't resist checking Ted's reaction to her
slim, fresh prettiness. If he noticed, she couldn't tell. He
held her hand, not as if he wanted to give her comfort,
but as if he were afraid of losing her.

Miss Harrington acknowledged their anxiety. "I
know how hard the waiting is. Let me say first that you
passed the most important test. You meet the agency's
standard as acceptable parents, and we would have no
hesitation in placing a child with you."

"But," Ted said.

"You might want to consider some other options.
You may not be aware of all the possibilities."

She was discouraging them. Rynna could see
￢ᵒh her charming manner, the talk of options. They
˙ ᵓ allowed to adopt a baby.

ᵗruth," Ted said. "Do you think we

.ild, you should never give up,"
/ "But if I were you, I would take a

Damn it! Jason again.

Rynna was too stunned to say anything else. She sat numbly while Miss Harrington listed their options. They might consider a so-called "unadoptable" child—an older or handicapped child. They could have their own baby—an option many adoptive parents didn't have. They should consult an expert to get a realistic picture of the risks. If they were determined to adopt, they could try private adoption.

Ted listened, asked a few appropriate questions, and thanked Miss Harrington for her time. He was scrupulously polite.

In the car, slowly coming to, she said, "You knew what she was going to say."

"Not all of it," he said. He put his arm around her. "I'm sorry. Anyway, we have Rob."

"Yes," she said. They should be satisfied, grateful. Rob was strong, healthy, and beautiful. She leaned against Ted while he drove home, and she said nothing at all. She couldn't explain the depth of her chagrin. He had no way to understand or share her feelings. He loved Rob, but he didn't want children in the abstract. He'd done his best, but he wasn't deeply sorry about their dashed hopes. Her resentment smoldered, and she dared say nothing she might regret later.

She went next door to pick up Robert and thank Fran and told her only that nothing was definite yet, which was true enough.

When she returned to the bedroom, Ted was changing into his old sweater. She laid Robert on the bed and smoothed his hair gently. He beamed up at her, and she gave him a finger to grasp. He was strong. He was going to be tall and handsome.

Ted sat on the bed and watched the baby. He didn't touch her. "Rynna? Are you going to talk to me?"

If she was going to feel like this, she should at least try. "You're relieved, aren't you?" she asked.

"Relieved? Jesus, Rynna."

"Aren't you?" she challenged him. "You didn't want—"

"All right," he said. He started to get up. That was like him. He would leave the room rather than fight.

"Ted, don't. I'm sorry. I didn't mean that. It isn't your fault."

"Yes, it is. That's what you think, isn't it? I won't give you a child, and because of me, you can't adopt one either."

"It's not because of you. It's not only…"

"I'm sorry," he said. "I thought you knew what you were getting into when you married me. I guess I was wrong. Maybe I should've spelled it all out for you. I promised we would try. I don't know what else I can do."

"Oh, Ted." Tears stung her eyes, but she didn't give way. He so hated her to cry.

"What do you want to do?" he asked. He looked as confused and unhappy as she was.

She lifted Robert and put him in Ted's arms. His face softened, but he knew what she was up to. Unfair tactics. His eyes were unguarded, but stubbornness showed in the set of his chin. "Couldn't we have another baby?" she coaxed. "Not right away. In a year or two."

"No."

"The first time wasn't so terrible, was it? All the things you worried about and look—he's perfect."

"Yes. We were lucky."

"So couldn't we—"

"No. I've read everything available on genetic factors in arthritis. I don't need an expert to tell me what the risk is. You don't know what it would be like. I won't do it." He wasn't angry, but he was absolutely determined. Arguing would do no good. He would leave her before he would abandon his long-held principle.

"What, then?" Miss Harrington had been bursting with options. "Do we try something else?"

"Whatever you want," he said.

Except what she wanted most. "What did she mean about private adoption?"

"Oh—find a doctor or lawyer who knows somebody, an unwed mother, pay her expenses, and arrange the adoption without an agency. If she doesn't change her mind at the last minute or have the same objections the agency did."

Rynna liked the simplicity of the plan. Maybe Dr. Moran or Dr. Zalman… "How were you adopted?" she asked.

"I don't know."

"How could you not know?"

"I just don't." He was slightly exasperated. "It's not important. What difference does it make?"

He had said the same thing about being adopted at all, and what a difference it had made in their lives. "But, Ted, you must know something. Didn't you ever ask? When did they tell you that you were adopted?"

"I don't remember being told. I always knew."

"You never asked for details?"

"What difference would it make?"

Rynna gave up. She would ask Dr. Moran. He might know about Ted's adoption, and he might know what they could do to arrange a private one. Deciding on one course of action, however tentative, eased her frustration. What else could she try? What were the other options Miss Harrington mentioned?

"What about—what did she say? Unadoptable children?"

"I'm willing, if you are."

"An older child? Older than Rob? Or wait a few years and adopt one his age or younger? When he's five, we could adopt a three-year-old girl." And miss the baby years? Miss what they were experiencing now with Robert?

Ted said, "I don't think that's what they mean by an older child. I think the unadoptable ones would be older—maybe ten."

Ten? She hoped he was wrong. They would be adopting a child who was half grown, with a personality already developed, warped by life's injustice, a child who remembered her own parents, or who had been shuttled from one foster home to another and trusted nobody.

"Think about it," he said. "Or a handicapped child?"

"Ted! Isn't that what you wanted to avoid?"

He shook his head. "Children who are already born, already disabled, who need a home. It's not the same thing. It wouldn't be easy, though. You might have enough to deal with as it is."

"After all this time," she said, "you still mystify me."

Much later, while she was undressing for bed, she said, "I don't think I could handle an 'unadoptable' child. Do you think less of me?"

"No," he said, with such immediate warmth that she knew he was sincere.

"I'm a selfish pig," she said. "I want what I want."

He stroked her hair. "So do I."

"I don't know," she said. "You're nicer than I am, I think. You've changed since I first met you."

"No, I haven't," he said, surprised by the direction of the conversation. He couldn't have been feeling at all generous, certainly not on the subject of her desire for children.

"Yes, you have. You used to be so…"

"Stubborn," he suggested.

"You still are. But more easygoing, less caustic. Am I embarrassing you?"

"Yes, you are. Anyway…" He gave her a quick kiss. "Everybody is nicer when they get what they want."

Chapter Sixteen

On Saturday, Mr. Baxter and a serious young accountant Rynna had never met showed up to discuss taxes with Ted. Rynna, sobered, reflected that something new would always come along to worry about. They had plenty of money, but most of the capital was tied up, and she didn't know anything about such matters—death duties, estate taxes? Ted was noticeably grim, which made her think she was right to worry.

His mood improved markedly after they left. He hadn't been worried, only bored and annoyed. Except for the recently discovered pleasure of buying things for her, money was of no interest to him, and at times like this a great deal of trouble.

A light rain began in the early evening and, instead of slacking off, increased steadily. Except for the occasional flash of lightning and crash of thunder, which she feared would frighten Robert, Rynna liked the storm. They were safe and warm inside their snug little house. Ted lit a fire in the fireplace, and she made oatmeal cookies and hot chocolate. They enjoyed a quiet, peaceful evening sitting by the fireplace, talking.

They didn't talk about adoption. Rynna still had a fresh ache in her heart, but she was too hopeful for depression, and nothing she felt now could be fully shared. They had so many other things to talk about— the house, Robert, the theory of ghost hunting, Ted's teaching. When he fell silent, staring into the fire, she was almost afraid to ask what he was thinking. What was he brooding about, the past or the future?

She touched his arm, and he raised his head. "Let's go to bed," he said.

The rain sounded even harder in the bedroom, where they could clearly hear the downpour buffeting the awnings. The thunder rumbled more frequently but didn't come any closer. They snuggled together under the blankets, sharing warmth and comfort. "I wish," Rynna said and didn't bother to finish the sentence. He knew what she meant. "Abstinence makes the heart grow fonder," she said.

"It isn't my heart you want," he said. "You have that."

"Theodore! What a thing to say." She was pleased, warmed. He said so little about his feelings, and yet he could be as sweet as this for no reason at all.

"Don't call me that," he said. He wasn't upset. The protest was habit now.

"Sorry," she said. Thunder cracked, too close for comfort, and she burrowed deeper under the covers. "Hold me, Teddy."

His arms tightened around her at once, but he said, "If you call me that again, I'll smack you."

"No, you won't," she said comfortably.

"Don't be too sure."

"I'm sorry. I won't say it again, but I know you won't hit me." It was unfair to tease him on this one subject when he never made a fuss about anything else, but sometimes she couldn't resist. "Why do you love me?" she asked, feeling a shade guilty.

"Why?" He was momentarily at sea. "Because

you're strong and brave, beautiful, intelligent, sexy, funny…"

"Am I?" she asked, humbled by such fine words.

"Because you're my best friend," he said. "Because you don't understand ionic bonding."

"Yes, I do, sort of," she protested, and while she was still laughing—

"Because I have no choice."

She fell asleep in his arms, lulled by the rain and the safety of being loved. She didn't wake until Robert cried. The rain had stopped, and the room was still and peaceful while she nursed him. She was a selfish pig to want more than this. When she had put Robert back to bed, she snuggled again against Ted and fell asleep at once.

She dreamed about the storm, the room lit up by jagged flashes of lightning, the thunder rumbling a background to the endless rain. She lay awake beside Ted, but he was far away. She was completely alone. The door was open, although she had shut it when she went to bed, and she knew who was out in the hall, waiting to come in. She couldn't reach Ted, couldn't speak to wake him. She wasn't sure she wanted to. Involving him might not be safe.

Jason stood in the doorway. The lightning flashed on his pale face and dark eyes, eyes like coal, black and empty. He said, "Rynna," clearly, distinctly. She remembered his voice so clearly. He beckoned.

"No," she whispered desperately. "No."

His eyes blazed. He marched into the room and reached inside his coat for the weapon she knew he carried—gun, knife? His hand came out…

"No!" She woke herself screaming, sat straight up in bed, and covered her face in terror of what she might see.

"Jesus, Rynna." Ted's familiar voice, his hand on her shoulder. She took refuge in his arms at once. It was a dream, only a dream, and it was over. The storm had ended. The room was quiet again, and a patch of moonlight glowed near the window. Ted was holding her. "Bad dream?" he asked, ready to sympathize.

"Yes," she said. She withdrew a little and brushed her hair back out of her eyes. She inhaled deeply and glanced around her safe, familiar bedroom.

The door was standing open.

****

Ted was sure they must have left the door open, but Rynna remembered closing it and seeing it closed when she nursed Robert. She hadn't locked it, but it had certainly been firmly closed. Ted couldn't let go of his skepticism. He believed, and he didn't believe. She still didn't know how he reconciled the apparition of Rosalind at Stonebridge with his rational convictions. Jason as emotional memory, as a divisive force in their marriage, as biological father—that was enough for him to deal with. Jason as surviving spirit? Maybe. Maybe her bad dreams were nothing more. But the candles…

Elaine hadn't been joking. She did have a Ouija board stuck away in a closet, and one cool, overcast evening she brought it to River Valley Road. Feeling foolish, childish, and self-conscious, Rynna helped Ted set it up on the changing table in the nursery. It wasn't ideal, but they would manage. Darkness had almost fallen outside, and with the light off, the room was shadowy and dim, not frightening but appropriately spooky. Elaine wanted to light candles—for more light, for atmosphere.

"Behave yourself," Ted told her.

They gathered around the board, Rynna and Elaine in dining room chairs and Ted in his wheelchair, and lightly touched the planchette with their fingers in approved fashion. Nothing happened. They got silly, teased each other, sobered, and tried again. Ted pushed back from the board and let the women continue. His skepticism might be in the way. The shadows lengthened, and finally it was too dark to see. With the light on, the room would be too bright, the mood too stark.

"Get the candles," Ted said finally. If they were going to do this, they would go all the way. One more time they would try to get some response, open their minds, sit quietly, and wait for something to happen.

With the candles flickering, throwing weird shadows on the board, Rynna felt the planchette shift under her hands. "Don't push it," Elaine whispered.

Rynna, dry-mouthed, whispered back, "I'm not."

X. The planchette quivered, hesitated under their fingers, and slid again. E.

Ted picked up his pencil and wrote the letters on the telephone message pad, large enough to read in the candlelit room. He wasn't thinking, wasn't passing judgment. They might as well document the experiment.

The planchette slid again. L. Swiftly, unerringly, back toward the start. A. X.E.L.A. Nonsense. Gibberish.

"Sounds like a radio station," said Elaine.

"No," Ted said. "Look." He wrote the letters again, this time right to left. A.L.E.X.

Rynna gasped. "Alex?" and seeing that Elaine didn't know what it meant, "That was Jason's father's name."

Elaine wanted to try again, but Rynna, shaken, was

reluctant.

"I think that's enough for tonight," Ted said. He didn't know what to make of the whole experience. The Ouija board was a children's toy. Eventually your own nerves would make something happen. Nothing happened with him. He wasn't suggestible enough, or he wasn't welcome here. Like the dreams, this originated with Rynna. In some way, unconsciously, she was making something happen. The phenomenon wasn't susceptible to independent scientific investigation, which was almost the same as saying it didn't exist, and yet...

Later in bed she whispered, "What do you think it means?"

"I don't know," he said, his voice muffled in her hair. "I don't have a clue."

She lay quietly in his arms, thinking her own thoughts, and he tilted her chin up to kiss her. "What was that for?" she asked.

"I just felt like it." He kissed her again. "Don't worry," he said. "We'll figure this out. We're just getting started."

Were they? Even as she responded to his kisses, her mind struggled with the problem. Why Alex? She had never known Alex, had never seen a picture of him except for the fuzzy one in the newspaper microfilm. He didn't resemble Jason particularly, but she didn't doubt he was Jason's father. And he had killed Rosalind.

Alex. X.E.L.A. Jason Alexander Wyatt.

She was on the verge of something, close to a real clue, a way to unravel the mystery, but the answer remained tantalizingly out of range. Still puzzling, she fell asleep.

****

When Rynna came out of the bathroom in the morning, Ted, sitting on the edge of the bed, half dressed, was taking a pill. She was too late to see which bottle he had taken it from.

"Ted?" She sat beside him, and he gave her a straight look, no evasion. She couldn't tell anything from his eyes. "Are you okay?"

"Sure. It's nothing."

"You always say it's nothing, even when I can see it isn't. If you don't tell me, I'll worry."

"Okay," he said. "I'm telling you. It's nothing." She still suspected he was brushing her off, but he might be telling the truth this time. He buttoned his shirt, and she rose and went to the dressing table to brush her hair. She studied him surreptitiously in the mirror and then realized he was watching her.

"You have beautiful hair," he said. It wasn't mere flattery. Was he trying to distract her? She smiled and kept brushing. Her hair was so long, so heavy, so much work to keep looking neat. But she couldn't cut it, not when he gave her such compliments. He got into the wheelchair. Yes, he was all right. The trouble was that she didn't know enough. He wouldn't tell her anything. She could do what he did—read a lot of books on the subject. But every case was different, and he would hate having her quote irrelevant generalities.

He said he had read everything available about genetic factors—probably too much. He had also said the unsuspected things were the scariest, so why balk over the one thing they were aware of? Her own genes might carry a few surprises, and who knew what else his might harbor? He had no family history.

"Ted, did you ever think of trying to find your—the woman who gave birth to you?"

He wasn't surprised. He was getting used to her unexpected questions. "No. The adoption records were sealed, and anyway I always sort of assumed she was dead."

"Really? Why?"

He shrugged. "Never thought about it. I guess...maybe because of what happened to Clara, I assumed she died in childbirth." Yes, that theory made sense but also conveniently ended all need to wonder where she was and why she gave him up. "What is this all about?" he asked.

Rynna shook her head, but she didn't stop thinking about it. What if his natural parents had kept him? What if he had been orphaned later, when he was older, after the arthritis began to destroy his knees? He would have been doubly "unadoptable." Ted, her Ted, with all she loved about him, unwanted? Appalled, she stared into the mirror, the brush frozen in midair.

"Rynna?"

She laid aside the brush and met his gaze. "Maybe we should think about an 'unadoptable' child after all," she said.

He didn't follow her train of thought, but he said, "All right, we'll look into it." He came and brushed her hair back from her face to kiss her. "But not this morning," he said, smiling. Did he think she would change her mind again, or did he mean not until they had laid Jason to rest? No matter. He kissed her sweetly. Too bad he had to work today.

****

After Ted left for class and the breakfast dishes were

washed, Rynna stood in the doorway to the nursery. She'd put a lot of loving care into the decorating. Now the room was empty, neglected, and a little dusty. The Ouija board was still on the changing table, folded in half, and it too had a neglected air. She wouldn't mess with it, not alone.

Her gaze fell on the rocking chair. It was damned unfair for Jason to scare her away from this. She and Robert had been so happy together in the chair, rocking gently. Why should they give up such a simple pleasure, even temporarily? Why couldn't they move the chair into the bedroom? She should have thought of it sooner. She should've done it when Ted was home to—what? Protect her? Foolishness.

Nevertheless, she lingered in the doorway. Why was the feeling so different when he was with her? Whatever she feared was intangible. He didn't know how to fight it. Skepticism was no protection. She wanted the rocking chair, and she marched into the room, grabbed it, and half dragged, half carried it out of the nursery. It wasn't heavy, but it was awkward. She didn't panic, but urgent haste made her clumsy. Once she was safely out in the hall, she relaxed and tugged the chair more slowly, more carefully, into the bedroom.

It didn't really fit. She spent about twenty minutes shoving the furniture around, trying to make everything work. When she was satisfied with the arrangement, she stood back to admire her handiwork. Yes, it was all right, except she had forgotten the wheelchair.

She could put everything back the way it was at first. If the room looked terrible, they would be even more motivated to settle the problem of Jason and get Robert back in the nursery where he belonged. She nursed him, comfortable and a shade defiant. Jason might force them out of the nursery, but he couldn't cheat them of their rocking chair.

When Robert was asleep, she went into the bathroom to wash her long hair. It was such a chore, but not as bad as when she was pregnant and couldn't bend over the sink. She should be thankful for small favors. She rinsed the last of the shampoo out and was briskly toweling her hair when she heard footsteps outside in the hall.

Rynna's heart skipped a beat. She wasn't imagining it. Someone was coming down the hall. Who? Ted couldn't have managed such an easy, confident stride. Nor was it George Archer's usual shuffle. Somebody was in the house, somebody who didn't belong, a burglar, an intruder.

Her baby was asleep in the bedroom, between her and whoever was walking so boldly toward her. Without thinking, she grabbed the nearest object—the hairbrush—to use as a weapon and ran out of the bathroom.

As soon as she emerged, the footsteps stopped. Nobody was there. The bedroom was empty. The hall was empty. Robert slept undisturbed. But she had heard them. They were real. "I'm not crazy," she whispered fiercely. "I'm not." She couldn't stand this. She couldn't live here if she continued to be tormented by dreams and strange noises and the creepy, restless sensation that consumed her now. It wasn't only that she had been frightened. It was something else. She couldn't stay here. Something was wrong here. She needed help. She needed to get out.

When it finally passed, she was lightheaded.

Anxiety attack? Or had something—or someone?—tried to communicate? The feeling of needing to leave, of something preventing her, something wrong—she shouldn't have such emotions standing in her own bedroom beside her sleeping baby.

Was this what Jason suffered? Did he want to leave as much as they wanted him to? What prevented him? What had they done wrong that he couldn't change and couldn't forgive? "Jason, please don't do this to me. I don't understand. Please."

Nothing happened. She began to feel foolish, with her hair tangled and wet and the hairbrush in her raised fist.

She didn't tell Ted about the episode. It was too intangible, too easily dismissed as her imagination. Whatever happened, she didn't want him to think, as Ian Wyatt did, that she ought to be locked up.

They did talk about Jason. Elaine was keen to try the Ouija board again, and Ted agreed, whatever his opinion of the first result. Elaine loaned him a book a friend had given her when he learned she had a Ouija board. He read bits of it aloud to Rynna, and they were sobered to know the author considered what they were doing dangerous and foolhardy. The board wasn't a toy, however much it might resemble one.

Still, if they couldn't communicate with Jason, how could they hope to deal with him? Something needed to be done. Elaine was busy tonight, but she promised to come over in a couple of days and try again. They couldn't go blindly in and haphazardly invite chaos. Ted thought the answer to everything was in books. He read a few more pages and gave the book to Rynna. "Maybe you and Elaine should try it without me," he suggested.

"You might get better results."

Rynna shook her head. "I don't want to. I want you there."

"Scared?"

"Yes. Maybe he doesn't want you there, but I won't face him without you. Never again." She shuddered with the memory of the last few times she was alone with Jason, of her terror of being beaten, choked, and finally of being touched at all. She gave Ted a piteous look. "Don't leave me alone with him," she said.

"Rynna." He was both moved and impatient. The way to settle this was to keep their heads and proceed logically. "He's dead. Jason's dead."

"I know," she said. What difference did that make? "I know he is. Does he know? I don't care if you think I'm being silly. I'm scared. I want this to end. I don't care how you do it. Just end it."

Chapter Seventeen

The next day, Rynna encountered another kind of ghost.

She had taken Robert into town. They did a little shopping, and both saw the doctor. Robert had a slight cold, nothing serious. In the drugstore near the university, while they waited for the pharmacist to fill the prescription, she pushed the carriage up and down the aisle to keep Robert from fussing. Only a few people were in the store at this hour, and she barely noticed them anyway. She was only half conscious of the slim, blonde woman selecting rolls of film at the next counter.

"Mrs. Demeray," the pharmacist called, and Rynna collected Robert's nose drops and wrote a check. As she left the counter, she realized the blonde woman was staring curiously. Rynna would have ignored her and gone out, but she was naggingly familiar.

"I'm sorry," she said, "Do I know you?"

"No, I—I didn't mean to stare. I heard him say your name was Demeray, and…"

Rynna remembered where she had seen her face before. In a photograph. It was Sylvia.

"I wondered if you were any relation to the Stonebridge Demerays."

"Yes. I'm Ted's wife. And you must be Sylvia Thompson."

"Quinn," she said. "It's—it's Quinn now." She

flushed. She must have realized that if Rynna knew her name, she knew more about her. "I'm sorry. I didn't mean to bother you."

"Not at all. Listen, do you have a minute? I'd like to talk to you."

"Oh, no, I—I don't think—"

"Just for a minute. A cup of coffee?"

Sylvia hesitated, glanced at the baby carriage, at Rynna's face. Curiosity warred with reluctance and finally won. "All right," she said.

At the busy, modernistic coffee shop across the street, they sat at a small table in a quiet corner. Sylvia ordered black coffee, and Rynna tea with lemon. "Do you mind if I smoke?" Sylvia asked. Rynna did, because of the baby, but Sylvia was nervous, visibly on edge, and might take off like a bird if she wasn't placated. Rynna shook her head politely, and Sylvia dug in her shoulder bag for cigarettes and lighter while Rynna studied her covertly.

What had Ted found so attractive? She had the same fine blonde hair as in the photograph, but not the sunny smile. She was so edgy, so brittle. Maybe the circumstances had unnerved her. She did have a pretty face, good bones, and fair skin. Her eyes were blue, and she had long eyelashes. Rynna couldn't help admiring her makeup, which was subtle and skillfully applied. Except when she used cosmetics as camouflage—to hide bruises or the ravages of sleepless nights—she preferred to wear only lipstick, but she was envious of the way Sylvia had used eye shadow and blusher to subtly enhance her natural beauty.

Sylvia took a long drag on her cigarette. "You said...you're Ted's wife?" She studied Rynna, curious and frankly appraising. What sort of woman had finally taken on the prickly, disabled scientist?

"Yes," Rynna said with a hint of smug pride. *Yes, he's mine now.* "He's teaching at the university."

"Ah." Sylvia was unsurprised and, in some way, pleased. "I read in the paper about his great-grandmother's death."

"Yes." Had she also read about Jason? "Do you live around here?"

"No. Visiting. I've been living in Washington."

"You're married now?"

Her long lashes shielded her eyes. "Divorced," she said. "How long have y'all been married?"

"Not long." It was her standard answer. The more people who assumed Robert was Ted's child the happier she would be.

Sylvia's gaze strayed to the baby carriage. "A boy?" she asked.

"Yes. His name is Robert. He's six weeks old."

"He's really cute." Sylvia was at a loss for words, but finally managed to say what she was thinking. "I didn't think Ted wanted to have children. He didn't when…when I knew him."

"No. He still feels the same way, I think, but he loves Rob. Babies are hard to resist."

"I suppose," Sylvia said politely.

"Don't you want children?"

"No, not particularly." Rynna could tell the question had calmed her as much as the cigarette. Ted hadn't told Rynna everything. "I'm sorry, I don't think you told me your name."

"Sorry. Rynna."

"Rynna? Pretty name. How did you recognize me?"

"I saw a picture of you once."

"Did Ted tell you we were…"

"Yes, but he didn't say much. You know how he is."

Sylvia smiled, and for the first time she resembled the vibrant girl in the photograph. "Yes, I remember. I hope y'all are happy."

"Thank you. Yes."

"I couldn't… I'm glad he found somebody. I couldn't manage it somehow."

Rynna had so many questions to ask, and she never could. Not even if they weren't strangers, not even if they were friends. She pitied Sylvia, who had lost whatever chance she'd had to be happy with Ted and apparently hadn't found happiness anywhere else either.

Sylvia knew she had said too much. She covered her embarrassment with small talk. The weather was always safe. "Who is at Stonebridge now?" she asked finally. "Are y'all living in town?"

"Yes. The house is ours now, but we're leasing it. We have a house near the university."

"It was a grand old place, Stonebridge," Sylvia said. "Did you know the old lady, his great-grandmother?"

"Yes. She was very kind to me."

"In her own way," said Sylvia. "I remember what she was like." She glanced up under her lashes and asked, a bit too casually, "Do you know Ted's cousin, Jason Wyatt?"

Too well, Rynna thought, with a shiver of remembered horror, but she said only, "Yes, I knew him."

"Is he still in Brenford?" She blew out smoke with studied nonchalance.

"No," Rynna said. "I'm afraid he's dead."

"He's dead?" She masked her shock with polite concern. "He wasn't that old. Not a heart attack?"

Rynna shook her head. "It was an accident."

"How dreadful," Sylvia said with bland sympathy, but she had given herself away. She was more interested in Jason than in Ted. She wished Ted well, but Jason was the one she had been waiting to ask about. Something in her manner, something unmistakable to Rynna as it might not have been to anyone else, told her Ted wasn't all they shared. She didn't know much, but she knew Jason and Sylvia had been intimate. Of course, some women would prefer Jason's charm and mastery, or maybe Ted and Sylvia simply hadn't loved each other enough.

"I won't keep you," Rynna said. She knew all she needed to know, and Sylvia more than she wanted to. "We have a few more errands."

"Yes," Sylvia said. "I'm meeting a friend in a few minutes." Her quick, guarded glance told Rynna the friend was male, more than a friend, and didn't belong to her. She was meeting a married faculty member, she guessed. So long as it wasn't Ted.

Was that a pattern? Sylvia didn't want the men she could have, wanted the men she couldn't have? Unfair to judge her on so little knowledge. She wished she knew what Jason had started to say about her, what he had almost called her. He had said, "She was a—She was smart and pretty, real class." Yes, she was classy—and a bit sad.

"I'll tell Ted," she began.

"Maybe you'd better not."

Rynna conceded the point. "Anyway, I'm glad we met."

She *was* glad. An astounding feeling welled up after she parted from Sylvia. She was no threat to their marriage. She wasn't even the woman Ted had once loved. His Sylvia was gone if she had ever existed. Ted was all hers, and Sylvia didn't know what she had given up.

She finished her errands and drove to the campus. Ted wasn't expecting her, but she didn't want to go home without seeing him. She left the carriage folded in the back seat and carried Robert to the geology building. She stopped at the office, where Elaine was diligently correcting papers.

"Hi," Elaine said, only a little surprised. "Are we on for tomorrow night?"

"Yes." She didn't want to think about ghosts and Ouija boards now.

Elaine raised her eyebrows. She could tell something was going on. "Does he know you're here?" she asked.

"No, it's a surprise. I'll see you later." She headed down the hall as classes were ending. The door of Ted's classroom was open, and students streamed out. A few hung around to talk. She stood back and waited until most of them passed. Her heart raced in an unexpected way. Wasn't she too married for romantic thrills?

Ted emerged into the hall, deep in conversation with a tall, gangly, graceless young man she remembered as a brilliant student. Ted glanced up and saw her and Robert, and his face lit up. He looked precisely the way she felt.

Rynna strode forward and bent to kiss him. She didn't even know if the student was still close. She didn't care, "Hi, sweetie," she said. "We thought we'd join you for lunch if you're not busy."

"Good idea," he said. His tone was a shade grim, although nothing had been lacking in his response to her kiss. She must learn to be more discreet, not to kiss him in public, not to call him "sweetie" even in private. She had resisted using endearments before they were married. Why did she find restraint so difficult now?

They ate lunch at an off-campus café frequented by faculty and graduate students. The place wasn't elegant or private, but neither of them noticed. They shared a plate of Louisiana shrimp with bowls of hot, savory vegetable soup. Ted didn't ask her what the doctor had said. He could tell by her demeanor. She explained about the nose drops and told him what she planned for dinner, while she studied his face and thought of Sylvia and what had once been between them. She didn't have the faintest twinge of jealousy. She was extraordinarily lucky.

She asked him what he'd lectured about and was pleased to understand most of the answer. What did Sylvia talk about with her "friend"? Did she understand his subject? Had she understood geology?

"You know," Ted said, motioning toward Robert in his carriage, serenely asleep, "Rob's old enough to leave with a babysitter now. We should go out more."

"Where?" Rynna asked, teasing. "Dancing?"

"If you like. Our social life stinks."

"I don't mind. I don't want to be with anybody but you."

"Thank you. But I would like to take you out."

"Where would you like to go?"

"I don't know," he said. "Paris?"

"Silly," Rynna said, but she knew he was serious. He would fly her to Paris if it would make her happy, if it would make her smile, keep smiling, never want to leave him. He knew she was restless sometimes. But it was Jason she needed to be free of. She wanted to tie herself more closely to Ted.

She had meant to say nothing about meeting Sylvia. She *would* say nothing. But when he was off guard, putting catsup on his French fries—not because he liked the taste, but because the bottle was in front of him—she attempted an entirely casual tone and asked the least casual of questions. "Ted, did Jason take Sylvia away from you?"

He raised his head, more than surprised. He couldn't see any connection between the question and their previous conversation, yet he couldn't have misunderstood what she said. His expression was curious and watchful. He could tell she knew something. But all he said, then or ever, was, "Not exactly." A minute later he had skillfully changed the subject, and Sylvia's name never needed to be mentioned again.

She wished they could say the same for Jason's.

****

That evening was more like a wedding night than their real one. Rynna spent hours on homemade pasta and a chocolate pecan pie to rival Mrs. Lester's, and chilled a bottle of champagne. Ted didn't approve, but she couldn't tell whether he disliked the alcohol or the sentiment. He could be so strait-laced sometimes, which was even more reason to get him relaxed, a little fuzzy. This wasn't a night to worry about anything.

She dressed in a new, lacy nightgown, suitable for a honeymoon. If he liked it, she would wear it every night—and hope the weather would soon be warmer.

"Very pretty," he said, when she came out of the bathroom, but she couldn't tell whether he meant it or only thought he should.

He was wearing his pajamas, as if nothing had changed and this was another night like any of the last three cool, rainy, sexless months.

"Do you love me?" she asked him as she unbuttoned his pajama top.

"You know I do."

"Really and truly?"

"Really and truly. Give us a kiss."

They kissed lingeringly, and she asked, "Why do people say that?"

"What?" He sounded as if he didn't much care.

"Give us a kiss."

"I don't know," he murmured against her hair. "I forget."

Yes, he had forgotten, and he would forget everything else too, everything except her. He couldn't forget her. She was in his blood, more intoxicating than champagne. He would always love her, and so long as they could be alone together at the end of the day, the rest of the world could never disturb them.

"Rynna," he said softly. "Rynna." Yes, sheer intoxication. She had missed this, the tenderness, his special sweetness, the touch of his hands, and here it was again, like an echo of memory, but real and immediate. Everything was as always between them, and in some indefinable way even better.

After passion, they shared contentment and laughter and the comfortable murmur of their voices in the darkened room. Rynna lay in Ted's arms, breathing in the scent of his skin, and said without thinking, "I never did this with Jason." It wasn't entirely true. It had sometimes been like this in the first weeks.

"I don't want to hear about what you did or didn't do with Jason," he said.

"Sorry," she murmured. She mustn't ripple these placid waters. She felt wonderful, beautiful, cherished. Ted's hand caressed her hair, so long now, dark and heavy and rich—for him, all for him.

"You have such beautiful hair," he said, and the words were more than flattery. It was almost a prayer.

Rynna grasped his hand and kissed the palm. "Do you remember the first thing you ever said to me?"

"No," he said. "Probably 'Hello.' "

"No," she countered. "The first thing you said to me was, 'You should let your hair grow.' "

"How polite. No wonder you didn't like me."

"It's all right, sweetie. I like you now." She reflected on those early days at Stonebridge and the strangeness of coming home as Jason's wife, of later discoveries, stolen kisses, the surprising passion for Ted, of leaving at last to marry him. "Do you miss Stonebridge?" she asked. How many years had he lived in that house? Most of his life.

"No," he said at once. "Why? Do you?"

"No, but I wondered if you did." She was silent again, dreaming in his arms. She had a new freedom and confidence in her own body, a wholeness she hadn't been aware of before. This was what she was made for—not to be used and sometimes abused by Jason, but to give to Ted, to share pleasure, to express love, to bear children.

No, she shouldn't be greedy. If they could adopt a child, he would welcome him or her as honestly as she would, but she needed to relinquish the idea of having another of her own. Robert should be enough for any reasonable woman. He was a miracle.

As if she had said his name aloud, the baby whimpered in his sleep and half awoke, fussing sleepily. She eased away from Ted and stroked a tiny shoulder. Robert shouldn't be hungry or wet and was too good a sleeper to be easily disturbed. She caressed his soft cheek and forehead. He wasn't feverish with his slight cold. He might be dreaming and want to be comforted. He responded to her touch, to her voice. "Hush, Rob Demeray," she whispered, "Daddy needs his sleep."

Presently he quieted, and she stretched out, close to Ted, but not touching him. He too slept peacefully. He had said he dreamed only of her. Her entire world was in this room—Ted and the baby. This was enough.

She slept and dreamed. Of Jason. He was angry, shouting, and she couldn't understand what he was saying, what she had done wrong. Why were their interactions always like this? Why was she always at fault? Why could he never listen, discuss things rationally, give her a chance to defend herself?

He grabbed her arm, twisted it, shoved her. Then his hands were at her throat, and he held her against the wall, his face close to hers, ugly and threatening. She wasn't so much frightened as wearied by the familiarity of all this. "Mine!" he shouted. "Mine. Mine." It was the one word she could understand, and so like him. Possession was everything. "Mine!" like a greedy, rebellious child, like an infant with no social sense. "Mine. Mine."

She called for help, for Ted. She had never been able to do such a thing before, in life or in a dream. She was always more fearful for him than for herself and never believed he had any power to fight Jason. But in the end, he had been strong, and Jason was the one who died.

Jason was dead. As soon as she formed the thought,

he was gone.

She awoke and breathed deeply. Safe, safe, with Ted, safe. Robert was awake and fussing again, not loudly. Ted stirred a little but didn't wake. Sleepily, Rynna reached a hand over the side of the bed to Robert's makeshift crib and murmured soothingly. Was he hungry? She sat up, on the edge of the bed between Ted and the nightstand so he wouldn't wake when she turned on the light.

She lifted Robert from the drawer and gazed at her beloved child. He was quiet now, eyes wide and alert, staring beyond her as if he saw something in the darkness beyond the lamplight. Without believing she would see anything, Rynna instinctively turned to look.

She leapt to her feet, terrified. The house was on fire. The baby protested and began to wail. She held him close and with the other hand shoved Ted's shoulder roughly to rouse him. "Ted, wake up!"

She looked again toward the door. Her first impression wasn't entirely correct, but something was certainly happening. Flames flickered at the edges of the door, which she had closed and locked to keep out phantoms. Was this a phantom? She didn't smell smoke. She could hear a hum, not the roar and crackle of fire, but something faintly electric. The light gave off no heat at all—she was cold right through and trembling. All around the door, licking futilely at the edge of the solid wood, the cold, white flame grew and spread, even along the floor, where it didn't singe the carpet.

Ted sat up and caught his breath in the sharp, pained way so distinctively his. "Cryptoluminescence," he said.

"What?" Rynna's heart was pounding. Was she seeing this? Even her dream was more real than this.

Least of all could she believe Ted would coolly face an inexplicable phenomenon and quote some babble from one of his wretched books. He glanced at her and slid out of bed, facing the door, unfazed by the weird light flickering on his face.

"Don't!" she cried.

He ignored her. Moving slowly—not that he *could* move quickly—he walked toward the door, touching the wall and then the dresser. When he was a foot away, he stretched a hand out to the mysterious light.

"Don't," she pleaded, certain the flames would hurt him, burn him if he ventured too near.

Heedless of her protest, he made contact with the fire—and it was gone.

Shaking with the release of tension as well as remembered fright, Rynna rocked Robert, her face bent over him. She refused to look at Ted. She was so furious, so terrified of what might have happened. What business did he have to take chances with things he knew nothing about?

"Rynna." He was beside her again, where he belonged, gathering her and the baby into his arms. "Are you all right?"

"Yes," she said. She took a deep breath and leaned gratefully against him. "Ted, weren't you even scared?"

"Yeah, I guess."

"What was that? What did you call it?"

"Cryptoluminescence. Unknown light. Something like that."

"Something like that?" She half laughed. "You are incredible."

"Me? Why? You didn't think it would hurt me, did you?"

"Yes! What caused it? What—?"

"You tell me." The edge of implication again, as if she were somehow responsible for the phenomenon.

"I dreamed about Jason," she admitted. "He vanished when I realized he was dead."

"Sounds like progress," he said. "But it doesn't look as if he liked it."

No, of course not. He didn't like her thinking he was dead. He didn't like her referring to Ted as Rob's father. No doubt he didn't like their making love, reclaiming each other. But he couldn't come in. They were safe behind the bedroom door. His rage might flicker around the edges, but he had no real strength, not if they didn't give in.

So, in defiance, as much as in desire, they made love again. Afterward, all was quiet and peaceful, and she didn't dream.

Chapter Eighteen

The following night, Elaine came over, and once again they solemnly set up what Rynna reluctantly labeled a séance. Ted lit the candles, in heavier glass than the first ones, to prevent flying slivers, and sat back to record the results. He took no active part, leaving Elaine and Rynna to rest their fingers lightly on the planchette and wait for a response. They waited so long Rynna grew drowsy, hypnotized by silence.

J. Ted wrote it down and they waited. Again, a long wait in almost perfect silence.

J. "Yes, Jason," Rynna breathed. "Tell us what you want."

Only a brief hesitation this time, and swiftly, unerringly, *My.* Then nothing, no matter how hard they concentrated, how tiringly long they waited. Nothing at all.

"That's so like him," said Rynna, when the lights were back on and they were trying sheepishly to return to normal. It was also like her dream—"Mine. Mine." She wasn't sure, from the dream and the timing of all these events, whether he wanted so desperately to claim her or her son or both.

****

For a long time, Jason didn't bother them. Rynna and Elaine used the Ouija board twice more, and nothing happened. No more unexplained lights, no extinguished candles, no mysterious footsteps. Nothing. For a long time, Rynna didn't dream of Jason or of Stonebridge. She dreamed prosaically of formula and diapers, of fabric for curtains, and of her husband, the geology professor. She was happy.

But she wasn't deceived. Jason wasn't gone. She still had a disturbed, restless feeling sometimes when she was alone, still preferred not to visit her beautiful nursery. She knew Ted was growing impatient. Keeping Robert always so close wasn't normal. It was more than a natural, protective instinct, more than any mother should be expected to feel. She couldn't blame Ted for his concern. He didn't think she was crazy, but she assigned these feelings too much importance, recovered too slowly from something he thought was over. He exercised restraint, tried to be patient. He even purchased a bassinet to replace the makeshift drawer bed. She tried to be tolerant of his feelings in return. He couldn't experience what she did. He hadn't belonged to Jason.

March came in like a lamb, and Rynna, driven by guilt and a hope of resolution, returned to the cemetery to visit Jason's grave. She hadn't been back since the funeral. The plot wasn't overgrown with weeds, but the grave had a neglected air. The stone wasn't impressive. Only his name and dates were engraved on it. "Beloved husband" would've been hypocritical and so would "beloved son." Poor Jason. Had anyone truly loved him for any length of time? Rosalind must have, when he was a child, but she had opposed him in the end.

Rynna left the grave a little more tended, bedecked with fresh flowers, feeling better for the deed. She had behaved for once like a dutiful widow, which was something she had never been. She had left to others both the responsibilities of his burial and estate and whatever degree of mourning had taken place. Ian might mourn him. She didn't. She wanted him to let go of her.

She had left the baby with Ted, and when she got home, they were in the nursery. Ted didn't share her irrational fears of the place. He sat near the crib, holding Robert, his back to the door, and didn't hear her come in.

Love for both of them welled up in her, overwhelming any lingering trace of guilt about Jason. What was so appealing about the back of Ted's neck, the way his straight blond hair lay against it? Why did it arouse these feelings in her—affection, tenderness, desire? She knew from a slight movement of his head that he was aware of her and bent swiftly to kiss the back of his neck.

"Hey," he said and looked up to smile at her, cradling Robert expertly in one arm.

"You're so good with him," she said, which was both true and a cover for her deeper feelings.

He was pleased. He so wanted to be a good father. He'd surrendered that desire long ago, and she had given it back. It was a gift, not the burden she had once feared. It didn't matter in the least that Robert was biologically Jason's child.

Except, of course, to Jason.

The peace continued for some time. The results she hoped for after her visit to the cemetery didn't materialize, but at least the situation grew no worse. The nursery began to have the neglected air of Jason's grave, even though Ted sometimes sat there with Robert, and Rynna was occasionally brave enough to carry him into the room when Ted was home. The baby still slept in their bedroom—a situation Ted continued to tolerate with watchful patience while he waited for her to come to her senses.

They made inquiries about private adoption and visited two orphanages to meet some of the so-called "unadoptable" children, and Ted waited for her to make some decision, to give him some clue to what she wanted. She didn't know what she wanted. Sometimes she was sure she wanted two children, not more than a few years apart, even if the only way they could accomplish it was to accept the terrible responsibility of a handicapped child, and sometimes she was equally certain these obstacles were meant to remind her Robert was all she needed. She mustn't coddle him, but he should have all the love and care she was capable of. He thrived on her care and grew stronger and more handsome every day.

He gained weight, slept through most of the night, and took pleasure in his bath. On fine days, he enjoyed being out in the sun. Every day he found some new discovery, some new delight. She didn't know who was more enchanted, she and Ted with the baby or Robert with his surroundings. They bought a collapsible playpen to use indoors and out and could both be absorbed happily for hours watching him discover his hands, his strength, his interest in the world.

He was strong and bright and sociable. He was a complete delight. He had almost too many toys. Ted couldn't stop acquiring one more bright object that rattled or flopped in Robert's eager hands.

One day he brought home a toy for Rynna instead.

He was strangely edgy all morning, and she wondered if he was in pain or catching a cold, although she had never known him to be really ill. He was impatient with her fussing and her delay over one thing and another, and she gladly left to run errands, leaving him with his books, his typewriter, and Robert.

When she returned, a piano stood in the living room.

It wasn't even her birthday, and his own birthday had passed with him insisting she not give him anything. He didn't want anything. She didn't want anything either. She certainly didn't need a brightly polished mahogany baby grand in the middle of her carefully planned living room.

Her first reaction was much like her reaction to the puppy. They couldn't do this. What was he thinking? How could he be so sensible and predictable most of the time and then do something so outrageous? What made him think she wanted a piano?

At the same time, a warmth was spreading in her chest. This was the wrong time, the wrong place, but she did want it. It was gorgeous. She hadn't played in so long. "Oh, Ted," she said, and he was so eager—between smug pride that he'd pulled off the surprise and anxiety that she like the gift—that she could only hug him and laugh. "Oh, Ted—yes, of course, but…oh, Ted!"

He had everything figured out, how the furniture could be placed to make room for it. The arrangement wasn't ideal. Someday soon they would have to find a bigger house to accommodate both the piano and his growing library.

"You're crazy," she said, but she trembled on the edge of happy tears. "I love you."

That was all he wanted—for her to love him—and she didn't need pianos for that. But now they would have music in the house. She would teach Robert to love music, real music, not tinny pop tunes on the radio. She would learn a few lullabies, and once again she would play Ted's favorites and her own and, if she dared, Rosalind's.

She was a little fearful that the piano, the medium of Rosalind's first contact with her, might in some way provoke Jason again. But she detected no effect, unless it was for the good, to soothe her when the restless, invasive sensation overcame her. For a while longer, the lull continued, and Jason didn't make himself strongly felt. Their lovemaking was a deterrent, a strength to use against him. So long as they were united, close in every way, he couldn't intrude.

For a while longer, safe in her house, her family, her music, Rynna was strong enough to withstand the nagging sense of something alien still within the house. She could take Robert into the nursery more often, although he still slept close to her at night.

As summer advanced, though, she began again to dream, in fear and confusion, of Jason at Stonebridge and on River Valley Road, threatening her or Ted, or trying to grab Robert. The restless feeling grew again, and fear returned to haunt the nursery and the front hall closet. She heard footsteps again and cowered in the bathroom, unable to face what she knew rationally must be nothing.

Ted was impatient with her and tried not to be. He had believed she was over this and didn't want to begin it all again. To convince him she wasn't imagining things and whatever was happening wasn't all in her mind, she insisted they try the Ouija board again.

Elaine was game. Ted shook his head, but set up the candles, four of them this time, lined up on the dresser. Once again, they waited a long time and finally, desperate to have some validation of her feelings, Rynna whispered fiercely, "Jason, darling, please let us help you." She closed her eyes and concentrated on nothing. She mustn't give in to the temptation to make something happen, to cheat. If she couldn't see the board, Ted couldn't suspect her of shifting the planchette deliberately.

The piece of wood stirred, and she kept her eyes closed. Elaine said, "J," and the brief scratch of Ted's pencil followed. "J" again and after a short pause, "My," a long interval during which they almost gave up, and "My" again.

"I know," Rynna said.

The planchette moved again, swiftly, almost slipping from her fingers. Swift, angry, definite. "My," Elaine said again, "My," and finally, faster and faster, "My son." While Ted was still writing, the candles blew out all at once, followed again by a shattering of glass, not so dangerously this time.

In the smoky aftermath, Rynna appealed to Ted for confirmation of her feelings. What was he thinking behind his poker face? Did he think she faked the message, even with her eyes closed? Was he upset that she appealed to Jason, called him "darling"?

No. "Jesus," Ted said. "Now what are we going to do?" This was what they'd feared most from the beginning.

Jason wanted his son.

****

Much of what occurred during the next few weeks was in the category of minor annoyances—flickering lights, vague sounds in the night, footsteps only Rynna could hear. Her dreams, though, were deeply frightening and grew uglier and more vivid all the time.

And then something else happened, something that took her mind off Jason and his threats. A vague suspicion slowly became a numbing certainty.

She was pregnant.

At first, she dismissed the possibility. They were so careful. *He* was so careful. She could think of only one possible time, but she had been so sure she was safe. She had assured him—oh, God! How many weeks ago? It couldn't be. She had still been nursing Robert. Surely, she was only overtired, nerves stretched by Jason's renewed annoyances. She couldn't be pregnant. As long as she didn't have a doctor's confirmation, she could pretend she wasn't sure.

She was sure. She carried the secret inside like an unexploded bomb. What would Ted say? "Get rid of it." As if a baby were a thing a surgeon could wrench out of her and leave no trace, as if the wrenching wouldn't be from her mind, her heart. What would it be like, to have life scraped out of her? How could he want such a thing? The operation was illegal and dangerous. He wasn't serious when he told her to get rid of Robert. He had taken care that she shouldn't face this dilemma. He wouldn't believe it was a mistake. What if he was right, what if all his fears were justified? What if this betrayal of his trust destroyed everything?

Then she entertained a guilty pleasure she was almost afraid to allow herself—What would Ted's child be like? Blond, blue-eyed, a slight cleft in its chin? Intelligent, naturally ironic? It would be such a pleasure to watch a child grow into small resemblances to Ted, a child created from their love, with their shared heritage. The Dalton and Demeray lines mixed with whatever ancestry Ted inherited—how to guess what the result would be?

Even if he wanted her to have his child, it was too soon. But she was strong and healthy. Bearing another child would be no burden. When? Next March? That wasn't so bad, was it? Fifteen months apart, close enough to be companions. They would have their family and no longer need to fight the adoption battle.

Ted could tell something was wrong, of course. But she could easily deceive him, for a while at least. He was used to Jason as a reason for her moods, her distraction. He was more than usually considerate and watchful. He suspected something, but she was sure he didn't suspect the truth.

She carried her secret, kept her silence, and she wept. Secretly, in the shower, silently in bed after he was asleep, alone during the day, she wept. She needed to confide in someone. She wanted to tell Elaine, but Elaine would never understand or forgive an abortion. She longed, for the first time in many months, for her mother. She conjured up the memory of mother-daughter chats, of her mother's warm, straightforward personality. She knew what Pamela would say: Tell him.

She didn't tell him, but she couldn't go on like this, not for long. She would be overwhelmed by contradictory thoughts and find herself standing over unwashed dishes or sitting stupidly on the unmade bed, unable to remember how long she had been there. She stood in the shower until the hot water ran out and bathed her face in cold water to cover the traces of her tears. She stared at herself in the mirror, searching for changes, signs of her guilty knowledge. Ted's child. What was she to do? Overcome, she sat on the edge of the tub, clutching her robe around her, shivering with something other than cold.

Chapter Nineteen

Rynna didn't realize how long she'd been in the bathroom until Ted rapped on the door and called, "Rynna? Are you all right?"

"Yes." She tried to sound normal, convincing. "Sorry, I'll be right out."

He was silent for a moment, and then he tried the doorknob. "Open the door."

"I'll be right out." She couldn't move. Her teeth were chattering.

"Open the door." He had never used so forceful a tone with her. It wasn't a command. It was something like desperation.

She opened the door. She was too close to the edge to meet his gaze. She retreated to the bathtub, shivering, and he came in after her. The bathroom was too small for both of them and the wheelchair. She wanted to smash it, as if it were the cause of his disability and not the means by which he moved beyond it. Worse, it was a symbol of the dangers he feared for their child. She was sick of it, sick of him, of herself, of thinking. She couldn't hold back the tears, tears he couldn't cope with and therefore hated.

"What is it?" he asked, trying to take her hands, to make her look at him. "Rynna, please, tell me." His voice was low, rough with fear, almost a whisper. "Whatever it is, you can tell me."

She raised her head, met the blue-gray eyes she loved so much. This was Ted, after all. She loved him. She took a deep breath. "I think I'm pregnant."

Whatever he was afraid of, that wasn't it. His immediate reaction was relief, but then he paled, his fingers tightened painfully on hers, and he said, "Christ, Rynna."

"I'm sorry."

"Are you sure?"

"No. Yes. Almost sure."

"Oh, Rynna…" He reached for her awkwardly in the cramped space, the wheelchair maddeningly in the way. He got out of it and sat on the edge of the bathtub, braced against the tiled wall, and gathered her into his arms. He held her close while she wept gratefully on his shoulder. A weight had been lifted. She was no longer alone with the secret.

He was silent, but she knew what he was thinking. He was counting back as she had, to that one night, that one lapse. He lifted her face to his, brushed tears from her cheeks. "I'm sorry," he said. "I was damn careless."

"No, oh, no. It was my fault."

He shook his head. "It was my responsibility. Christ."

"I thought you would be angry with me. I was sure you would think I got pregnant on purpose. I didn't, Ted."

"I know you didn't." His initial reactions—relief, shock, remorse—gave way to a deeper dismay. "Christ!"

She couldn't stop the tears, couldn't think what to say to help him.

"Don't cry," he said.

"I'm sorry." She took a shuddering breath and wiped

her face with the backs of her hands.

"It doesn't help," he said. She didn't know if he meant her tears or her apology. He slipped one hand inside her robe to rest on her still-flat abdomen. "How long have you known?"

"A few days. I wasn't sure."

"I mean how far along are you?"

"I don't want to have an abortion," she said, sure he was headed in that direction. She meant to say the words calmly, as if this were a rational, well-thought-out decision, but they spilled out in a fierce, passionate whisper.

"No, of course you don't. Did you think I—?"

"Yes! When I told you I was pregnant the first time, you said—"

"Jesus, Rynna! You never listened to me. You never took anything I said seriously. What difference did it make what I said? I knew you wouldn't pay any attention."

She was momentarily speechless. She took his hand. "That isn't true. You were my friend."

"I would have kept my mouth shut if I'd known you were going to hold my words against me for the rest of my life."

"I'm sorry, sweetie."

"Don't be sorry. And don't call me sweetie. Jesus, this is a hell of a note. I thought you and Jason were stupid to have a baby by accident. That's a scientist for you. In the end, we rely on luck like everybody else."

"You're a geologist," she reminded him. "What do you know about biology?"

"Don't get smart," he said. He cradled her close, comforting her, which wasn't at all what she had expected. She felt guilty to be so happy, to experience a surge of euphoria under her concern for him. She was sorry for the pain she had caused him and the pain he was sure to suffer in the future, but he wasn't angry. He would let her have his baby.

"I think you're taking this awfully well," she told him.

"Am I? I got you into this. The least I can do is let you be happy about it if you can. Life won't do you many favors, you know. You have to take what you can get."

She kissed him for that bit of philosophy.

"Jesus," he said. "We have all that to go through again. Isn't it dangerous to have another baby so soon?"

"It's not that soon. Robert will be walking by then. You mustn't worry, Ted. Last time everything went fine, and the second time is usually easier."

"I know, but I don't want you to suffer."

"I didn't suffer. You did."

He didn't answer. He held her, thinking his own thoughts.

She sighed. "I wish you wanted the baby as much as I do."

"Don't worry about it. I'm a slow starter, but I get there in the end. This is enough, though. Two was what we agreed on in the beginning. No more."

"Yes, two is enough."

"No more pressing our luck. I'll have a vasectomy. Locking the barn door. I should've done it in the first place."

"Why didn't you? Chicken?"

"Yes, but not the way you mean. I'll probably be sorry for telling you this."

"What?"

"I was afraid we wouldn't be able to adopt, and in the end you would talk me into this."

"Really? I never thought I could."

"You don't know your own strength."

"In that case you'd better hope I'm pregnant, or I'll make your life miserable until I am."

"Shit. I knew I would regret telling you."

Rynna laughed and kissed him. "Thank you for being so—"

"Don't you dare say 'sweet.' "

"Understanding."

"Why shouldn't I understand? I know I'm hard to live with sometimes, but I love you. Don't be afraid to tell me things. I'm not Jason."

Rynna stiffened involuntarily. She had forgotten Jason. With a little shock of recognition, she remembered that the renewal of hostilities had begun the day after this baby had likely been conceived. Did Jason know before she did? Now that she was going to give birth to Ted's child, was he more determined than ever to claim his son?

****

Ted was teaching in the summer quarter but had a light schedule. He was home more, and they began to go out again. Sometimes they left Robert with Fran, which Rynna tried not to mind, and sometimes they took him along. She was often relieved to get out of the house, where Jason was always waiting.

They began again to hunt for a house. The house on River Valley Road would be big enough for a long time yet, which gave them the freedom to take their time and search for something perfect. Rynna was determined not to let Jason drive them out. They would have to settle with him first.

They used the Ouija board again, with some reluctance and with much the same results. *J* repeated several times and insistently, *My.* "He hasn't changed," Rynna said.

She told Elaine about the baby, and she was both pleased and envious. They didn't tell anybody else, but word got around somehow. A more welcoming attitude grew among the other faculty and their wives. With Robert old enough to leave with a sitter and her new pregnancy not yet advanced, they couldn't avoid most of the faculty functions. She would never enjoy them, and Ted certainly didn't, but they became less of an ordeal. The other wives had forgiven her sensational past and radical ideas now that she was carrying Ted's child, the legitimate child of a respected professor.

She couldn't tell what Ted thought about the baby. He said little, but sometimes she caught him watching her when he thought she wouldn't notice. For the first few days, while the shock was still wearing off, she sensed a distance between them. After that, things were as before, and she was sometimes aware of a deeper tenderness in the way he caressed her.

If he didn't like the idea, he was nevertheless affected by the knowledge that this was his child. Sometimes in bed he would hold her reverently, his hand on her belly. Once, touched and curious, she asked what he was thinking.

"Nothing," he said. "I just feel very…married."

He never reproached her, never showed signs of resenting her part in their carelessness. She hoped he was more than resigned to the idea and would eventually welcome the baby as much as she did.

Once again, Rynna put much of her energy into decorating ideas. She planned to redecorate the nursery for the new baby and make a room for Robert in Ted's study. She still wanted Rob close at night, but it was time to make a change. She chose blue curtains and wallpaper with a giraffe motif and purchased a second-hand crib, knowing they would soon replace it with a toddler bed. He was growing up so fast! It was a little crowded with Ted's desk and full bookshelves, so she would postpone creating a play area until they found a larger house.

The first time she put him to bed in his new room, she was in with him half the night, unconvinced he would be safer than in the nursery. Jason might still find him.

Ted was first impatient and then sarcastic. "Jason is dead," he said finally.

Rynna's voice rose, heedless of the sleeping baby. "Stop saying that."

"Stop being hysterical, then."

"I'm not hysterical. I want to be sure he's all right. I'd rather have him in here, but I know you don't want—"

"I didn't say—"

"You don't have to. I know he's better off in his own room, but I want to be sure he's safe. If you felt the way I do about him—"

He stiffened. "Are you saying I don't?"

Rynna took a deep breath. "No. I'm sorry, I didn't mean that. What are we fighting about?"

"I don't know," he said, as close to sullen as she had ever seen him. "Nothing."

"Please be patient with me, Ted. Just for a few more days."

"Sorry," he said tersely. She wanted to kiss him, but in his present mood she might be risking a rebuff. She left the room again to check on her baby. Their baby. Jason had no rights. He was dead.

In a few days, as she had predicted, she adjusted to the new arrangement. If Robert cried in the night, she would force herself to lie still, to identify the sound as hungry or fretful, to let him cry if he didn't seem frightened. As far as she could tell, Jason didn't bother him.

He continued, however, to bother her.

One day she went into the nursery to get a few of Robert's clothes from the dresser drawers. They were gradually relocating everything to the other room, except for the things they would keep for the new baby. When she started to leave, the temperature abruptly dropped, and the door slammed in her face.

Rynna screamed. She remembered the awful coldness in the hall at Stonebridge before Rosalind appeared and stared around wildly for an apparition she feared to see. She saw nothing, but she knew she was trapped, alone, with something that wished her no good.

Ted wrenched the door open, with more force than should've been necessary. It wasn't locked but didn't give easily. "What happened?" he asked. He looked as frightened as she was but relaxed as soon as he was sure she wasn't hurt.

"The door slammed," she said inadequately.

He checked to see if the window was open. "Don't look at me like that," he said. "I believe you."

"Ted, what if it isn't safe in here for the new baby either?"

"Jesus," he said. "I've had about enough of this."

233

She wasn't sure whether he meant Jason's nonsense or hers.

Jason's. Ted delved into the books again and read her bits of theory—ghost as emotional memory, ghost as the non-physical factor in human personality. He talked more and more about their need to communicate. Rynna couldn't see how they could communicate to Jason what he refused to understand. With the Ouija board, they could receive communication from him, but he would only stubbornly repeat his unacceptable claim.

At Ted's insistence, she would sit in the nursery for long periods of time, sometimes in the dark, sometimes with the candles lit, until the smell of melting wax sickened her, and the restlessness drove her out. Sometimes she would start crying for no reason. "I don't want to do this anymore," she said after the last session. "It doesn't work anyway."

"We have to do something," Ted said.

"You mean I have to do something."

"All right," he said. "We'll move."

"No, he's not going to drive us out. Besides, he'd probably follow us."

Ted closed his mouth on whatever he was about to say and ran his hand through his hair. His patience was stretched to the breaking point. He pivoted away from her and returned to the books.

He tried everything he could think of. He repeated rituals they had tried before, with no more success. He said prayers, sprinkled holy water, checked out the credentials of experts he was still reluctant to call in. He insisted she try to communicate with Jason and couldn't understand her reluctance. Finally, he said, reproachfully, "You used to be in love with him."

"And you'll never forgive me?"

"No, I didn't mean that. But you should be able to remember loving him. Try to sympathize, can't you?"

She couldn't. She didn't understand how *he* could. His sympathy for Jason, always so rare, never failed to surprise her.

Ted acknowledged the incongruity. "The poor bastard was in love with you, and he can't have you. I know what that's like."

So she tried again, forced herself to stay in the room under unbearable tension. The most she ever achieved was a few seconds when she was suspended in time and space and blurted out, "It's not right." She didn't know what the words meant, and she was too unnerved to try the experiment again. "I'm not a medium," she said. "I can't get through to him. I'm not even sure I want to."

She dreamed about Jason more and more often. In one particularly vivid dream, she held the new baby—a girl in a frilly pink dress—and Jason had Robert. He was saying she couldn't keep them both. She put the baby on the cold, hard floor and held out her arms for Robert. He was her firstborn.

Shaken by the dream—every implication, every explanation she considered was worse than the last—she began occasionally to use sleeping pills, prescribed by Dr. Moran, who warned against taking them too often. She had always hated them, but she was desperate.

She continued to leave Rob in his own room at night but was no less anxious for his safety. She didn't know how to protect him. She didn't know what Jason was capable of.

While she did her housework, she would sometimes feel a need to go to him, even when he was asleep or in his playpen in the backyard with Ted nearby. She must be watchful. She mustn't lower her guard.

He grew big and strong and active, and she could foresee the time when he would be able to travel beyond her reach. Before he did, she wanted to make sure he wouldn't head into unseen danger.

One day, when she felt compelled to leave the breakfast dishes and check on him, Ted was in his room ahead of her. Robert was asleep, peacefully enjoying his morning nap, and Ted sat close to the crib, watching him. Rynna stood quietly until he raised his head. He had tears in his eyes.

"What is it?" she whispered.

He shook his head and looked back at the baby. He touched a small foot, ran his fingers gently over a dimpled knee. He said nothing, but she knew what he was thinking. Life held no guarantees. Rob might not always be so strong, so whole. Anything could happen to him. Whatever dangers Ted could imagine for him, still more lurked for the child of their union.

With a sigh, he removed his hand from their sleeping son and placed it on the slight swell of her abdomen. She had begun to feel life in the last few days, still too tentative to share.

"I know," she said.

"I'm really scared," he admitted.

"I know," she said again. "I am too. Hostages to fortune."

"Yes," he agreed. "Hostages to bloody fortune."

Chapter Twenty

On a rainy evening in October, Rynna sat playing the piano while Ted watched Robert, who was now crawling everywhere and could haul himself to his feet by holding onto the coffee table or the wheelchair. She played songs Pamela had liked and mused with nostalgic wistfulness on her childhood and the grandmother her children should've known.

"What's the matter?" Ted asked when her fingers fell idle on the keys.

"Nothing. Just thinking. I wish they were all here, all Rob's grandparents. They're missing all this."

"You're feeling blue tonight," he said. "Why?"

"No reason. The weather, I guess."

"Play something lively. Cheer us all up."

She did—it didn't help her mood—and then she played Brahms's lullaby. "Time somebody was in bed," she suggested.

Ted picked Robert up, and he protested. Rynna had begun to dread sleep and was determined not to communicate her fear to him. She wanted him to be as strong and happy and independent as they could teach him to be. Having him grow away from her was hard, but she was fascinated by the development of his individual personality. She could see, so far, no trace of Jason in him. She was comforted to know she would have another baby to hold in her arms when this one insisted on walking away from her.

She stayed at the piano and played snatches of half-remembered songs, while Ted put Robert to bed. She had overcome her concern about his ability to cope. Their little family was well established now, and their marriage was secure. They could be so happy, if only they could rid themselves of the stubborn shade of Jason Wyatt. How could she know, on those nights when Robert woke crying in the dark, whether he faced ordinary baby fears, or whether he dreamed of terrors he couldn't understand?

When Ted returned, his face was curiously alight. He left the wheelchair and sat next to her on the piano bench. "What happened?" she asked, touching the hair at the back of his neck.

"Called me 'Da'," he explained, pleased and a bit sheepish.

Rynna smiled quickly to cover her first reaction—*Jason won't like that*. She ran her fingers over the keys. "What shall I play?"

"Anything. Wait." He put his hands on the keyboard beside hers. "Chopsticks." They played the simple piece—not well—and Rynna laughed. He was trying to cheer her up. "It's wonderful to be able to play the way you do," he said. "I really admire your talent."

"You play great typewriter," she said. She so wanted to enjoy these small pleasures—music, quiet evenings, shared jokes. But she was so tired all the time and tired of being tired. Sleeping during the day didn't work. If Ted was home, she didn't want to nap, and if he wasn't, she was too nervous to relax. She couldn't sleep through the night without pills and disliked depending on them. She was often too tired to make love. Ted was patient, and she minded his patience more than his occasional bitter edginess. He had again suggested she see the psychiatrist. He might have helped her sleep or cope with the nightmares, but what could she say? That she was still obsessed with her dead husband?

No. She no longer considered him her husband. He was the enemy. Ted was her husband. They had been married twice as long as she'd belonged to Jason. Ted had proposed in the first place at least partly to free her from Jason, and he still hadn't done so. He didn't know how. The solution was up to her, but she couldn't find the answer.

"Are you all right?" he asked.

She drifted, brooding over the keys. Tears stung her eyelids. He was so good to her, and she was so helpless. She began to play, "You Are My Sunshine." Skies were gray, and he couldn't make her happy. But he would keep trying. He wouldn't take her sunshine away. At the end of the sprightly tune, she leaned in and kissed him. They could be so happy, if only…

He put his arm around her, lifted her chin, and kissed her, not casually, as she had kissed him, but seriously, intensely. She shivered with longing and anticipation, but she was so tired.

"It's all right," he said gently. "I don't ever want you to feel—"

"No, Ted, I—"

"—pressured or obligated. I'm not…" He didn't finish. The time had come to stop saying what they both knew. Jason was still in the way.

"I love you," she said. She put her hand on his left knee, and his fingers closed on hers.

"Come on, play something pretty," he urged.

At least she could smile and play the piano and

pretend Jason wasn't driving her to the wall.

Before they went to bed, she checked on Robert. He was fine, sleeping peacefully, one hand tucked under the soft roundness of his cheek. A beautiful child, perfect, whole, breathtakingly sweet and vulnerable. Uncontrollable emotion caught at her throat. She would never give him up.

She usually left the door ajar, the better to hear him in the night, but tonight, for some reason, she wanted to close it firmly, to shut out unsuspected dangers.

"Okay?" Ted asked when she came into the bedroom. He might think she was foolishly overprotective, but he wasn't immune to such feelings himself. *Hostages to bloody fortune.*

"Yes." Still on edge but comforted. "I don't want to take any more pills. No more pills." She climbed into bed beside him.

"No. It can't be good for the little one." His hand rested on her abdomen. She needed to take care of herself, for his sake, for their baby. "If you can't sleep," he advised, "or you have a nightmare, wake me up."

"I will," she said, although she didn't intend to. She saw no point in wearing them both out. She was awake for a while, listening as his breathing grew more even. Knowing he was safely asleep soothed her, as if it were somewhere he could go and be secure. If only she could follow him so easily.

She slept poorly and awoke restless and vaguely frightened. She slid carefully out of bed and checked on the baby. He was all right. He slept as Ted did, deeply and untroubled by dreams. When she came back to bed, Ted murmured sleepily and took her in his arms. She couldn't tell if he was awake or not.

She slept again and dreamed of a too familiar scene. Again, Jason demanded she make a choice. He held Robert, wrapped in a blanket, not sleeping, but strangely still. "No," she insisted. "You can't have him."

He loomed closer, red-faced and scowling, his voice rising. She wanted to tell him not to wake the baby, but Robert wasn't asleep. His eyes were open, and he gazed at her, waiting for her to act. Jason put his hand on her belly, not the way Ted did, not with tenderness or pride. He threatened her. She couldn't have them both. She mustn't be so greedy. If she wouldn't give Robert to him at once, freely, by her own choice, he could more easily deny her the other child. "Little Demeray bastard," he sneered. "It's going to be a cripple anyway."

She woke up absolutely terrified. This was the one thing he could do to her, however limited his power was. If she continued this way, if she couldn't sleep through the night without pills, she would lose Ted's baby. Jason could make her lose this baby.

No, damn it, she wouldn't let him. She would fight him on all fronts. She didn't need a sleeping pill. She only needed to make sure Robert was all right. As she hurried to his room, her heart began to pound with fearful anticipation. This powerful sense of something wrong was new, not lingering from the dream.

The hall was totally dark, darker than it should have been. She put her hand to her face to be sure her eyes weren't closed, and then suddenly there was light, more light than she wanted, enough to hurt her eyes. It ran all along the edges of the closed door to Robert's room, a cold, flickering, electric light, flame-like but without heat, the same phenomenon that had occurred some months ago in their bedroom—what Ted had called "cryptoluminescence."

Jason was trying to get to his son. She gulped and put a steadying hand to her heart. She wouldn't wake Ted, and she wouldn't retreat, and she wouldn't give in to horror. The first time, Ted had touched the light, and it had vanished. She could do no less than try.

She stretched out her hand, steeled herself for she knew not what, and made contact. Her fingers tingled slightly, and the line of flame was extinguished all at once. She jerked open the door. Inside the room was another sort of light, a faint, unearthly glow. She didn't want to know what it meant, what it might do. She snatched Rob out of his crib and ran out of the room. He had been asleep, but he woke at once and began to cry. She didn't blame him.

She slammed the door of the bedroom, locked it, and barely restrained herself from moving the dressing table in front of it again. Trembling, her heart pounding, she took Robert to bed with her.

Ted sat up and turned on his lamp. He could hardly have slept through the baby's screaming and her slamming the door. "For God's sake," he said.

"Light," she stammered. "In the—"

"Take it easy," he said. "You were dreaming."

"N-no, I wasn't. It was like before—fire around the door—and it was—"

"Take it easy," he said again.

Rynna took a long, shuddering breath, steadied, and regained her balance. She leaned back against the headboard and hugged the baby to her chest, trying to quiet him. He wouldn't be comforted. He screamed, his face red with a frightened rage he hadn't shown since he was much younger. Ted would say she was communicating her fear to him. He was still a part of her. Jason hadn't awakened him. She had.

"Jesus," Ted said. "We're back where we started."

Yes, back where they started, unable to leave the baby alone in another room, back to makeshift arrangements. Robert was too big now for a drawer or a bassinet, and the crib wouldn't fit. She held her screaming child and hovered on the edge of real and final despair.

"Rynna, can't you—?"

"No!" she snapped. "I'm trying. If you don't like it, go sleep on the sofa."

"Hey," he said, surprised and not at all defensive. "Here, give him to me."

She didn't like the implication that she wasn't capable, hadn't done everything possible, but yes, all right, let him try. He couldn't quiet Robert either, but at least he could take over for a while. She lay back, exhausted, her nerves raw, and listened numbly to her son crying and crying and Ted's voice, a futile litany against Rob's persistent outrage. "Hush, Rob, shh, you're all right." She didn't expect to sleep. She might never sleep again.

Worn out, stretched to the limit, she slept.

When she woke again, light flooded the room, the soft, natural light of early morning, remarkably quiet and peaceful. She stirred, and the baby moved inside her, more definitely than before. A reminder, a reassurance. They had at least survived this night. Ted was asleep, half sitting up against the pillows. Robert was asleep too, snuggled comfortably against his father's chest.

As she watched, he moved, stretched, and opened his eyes. She smiled, and he beamed back. She held out her arms, and he crawled up to put his sweet baby fist in her face. She laughed softly and lifted him in the air. He was growing so heavy, so strong. He smiled and cooed. "Shh," she whispered softly. "Daddy needs his sleep."

"Daddy is awake," Ted informed her.

"Da," Robert affirmed.

Rynna sat up. She'd enjoyed several hours of unexpectedly deep sleep, but she was tired, depressed, and discouraged. They were losing the battle with Jason, and she didn't know what else they could do. This was sweet—all her family together in the warmth of the bed, but the moment wouldn't last. All too soon she would have to get up and carry Robert to his room to change and dress him. She didn't want to go back, and she didn't want to admit her cowardice. She was thoroughly sick of living on these terms.

"Did you sleep?" Ted asked.

"Yes. Did you? You look uncomfortable."

He ignored her question and glanced at the clock.

"Don't go today," she said. "Elaine can take the lab."

"She has better things to do." He started to get out of bed, moving slowly, stiffly.

"No, you shouldn't."

"Rynna, please don't make a fuss." He went into the bathroom, and she lay back, resigned. She wasn't much good to anybody. Ted didn't need her. She was a burden.

"Da," said Robert, tugging her hair.

"All right, all right." Wearily she rose, donned a robe, and carried him into his own room, which was undisturbed. She was a little apprehensive but sensed none of the restless, oppressive atmosphere of the nursery.

She dressed him in her favorite outfit, a yellow plaid romper. He was ravishing, which at least cheered her up. He was such a handsome baby, with his pink cheeks and dark hair, and beautifully behaved most of the time. She warmed a bottle and returned to the bedroom to feed him.

She was sitting on the bed, cradling Robert in one arm, while he clutched the bottle and eagerly gulped formula, when Ted emerged from the bathroom, shaved and dressed. He sat beside her and brushed her hair back from her face. "You look tired," he said. He sounded as discouraged as she was.

"I'll live," she said. "At least Robert is thriving."

"Why don't you go back to sleep if you can. I'll give him his cereal and fruit."

"Thank you, sweetie. I can manage."

"Rynna," he said reproachfully.

"Oh, Ted, really!"

"That's better," he said, mollified, and kissed her.

"I don't see why you care so much what you're called. 'Ted' isn't all that exciting, you know."

"No," he said, "but it's who I am."

"No, it isn't. It's only a name. Names are only words. A rose by any other name."

He shook his head. He had a familiar, stubborn expression, the Demeray look. "Names aren't just words," he said. "They're part of your identity."

She shook her head. Most people acquired their names or nicknames by accident. "You let Grandmother call you 'Theodore,' " she pointed out.

"As if I could have stopped her. It was part of our relationship. 'Theodore' was who I was to her, and she never liked nicknames. When she called me 'William,' it was because he was part of my identity too. She

245

thought of me primarily as his son."

"This is too much analysis for me so early in the morning," she said. "I still say it's only a name, a convenient label for people to use, like any other word."

"No," he said stubbornly. "Your name is part of who you…" He was suddenly alert, as if listening to something a long way away. His fingers tightened painfully on hers. "Jesus Christ," he said.

"Ted," she protested. He was hurting her and unaware of it.

"Oh, sorry," he said, but his mind was somewhere else. He got out of bed and grabbed the wheelchair. For the first time, she sensed his impatience with his own limitations. He couldn't move fast enough to keep up with his racing mind.

"What is it? What's wrong?"

"Jesus Christ. Rynna, never mind the bottle. It'll wait. Take Rob to the nursery."

She had no intention of doing any such thing. *It'll wait*, indeed. Robert would have something to say about that. She wouldn't take him into the nursery, not without a damn good reason. It wasn't safe.

Ted rummaged through drawers, searching for something. He had apparently taken leave of his senses. "Did you hear me?" he asked when she didn't rise.

"I don't want to."

"Do it," he said. He found what he was looking for—the vial of holy water left from so many hopeless attempts.

She wasn't going through any more rituals, and she wouldn't take Robert anywhere near the nursery. If Ted wanted to confront Jason, he could do it alone. She remembered the dream she'd had some months ago, when she had carried the baby out of the room where Ted and Jason were quarreling so they wouldn't disturb him. She had the same instinct now.

Ted gave her an impatient but understanding look. "Trust me," he said and left the room.

She trusted him. She took Robert to the nursery. Ted was ahead of her, lighting candles in a row on the dresser. Her heart sank. She was sick of séances and Ouija boards and attempts to communicate with whatever part of Jason still lingered. She didn't want to be here, and she didn't want her baby here.

Finished with the candles, Ted closed the door. The Ouija board was not in sight. "Sit down," he said. He took the baby from her, oblivious to his fussing. No doubt Robert didn't like this place any more than she did. Ted laid him on the changing table. "Concentrate," he said. "Get Jason's attention."

She entertained horrible thoughts—of Solomon proposing to divide the baby, of Abraham offering Isaac on the altar as a sacrifice. "Trust me," Ted had said. She closed her eyes and was at once overcome by the vivid sense of Jason's restless spirit.

When she opened her eyes, the candles were flickering, casting weird shadows on the walls.

Robert started to cry.

Ted uncapped the vial of holy water, and as if in response the candles guttered and nearly snuffed out.

"I don't like this," she said.

He ignored her. He whispered soothingly to Rob, without much result. He sprinkled holy water on the baby's forehead and made the sign of the cross.

Only then did Rynna understand what he was about to do.

"In the name of the Father, the Son, and the Holy Ghost," he intoned, "I christen thee Robert Jason Alexander."

For a single breathless pause, nothing at all happened, and then the candles stopped guttering, the flames straight and steady. One by one, beginning with the one farthest from the door, they went out.

Rynna stood and picked up the baby.

He had stopped crying, and he put his thumb in his mouth.

Behind her the door clicked open. As she turned, it swung wide, slowly and entirely of its own accord.

Ted opened the curtains, and sunlight spilled into the room.

It was again the attractive, comfortable nursery she herself had decorated.

Could the solution be as simple as that?

Ted rolled out to the hall, and she followed, still a little dazed. The door of the hall closet stood open. Nothing lurked inside. The front door swung open.

Jason was gone. The feeling of restlessness, of something waiting and watching, had vanished. The sensation wasn't simply absent, but completely gone, in the way a pain is gone when you know it won't come back. The ordeal was over.

Jason was dead.

****

A few days later they learned the investigation of Jason's death had been officially closed. After more than a year, the timing could hardly be coincidental. In something like gratitude, Rynna paid another visit to the cemetery. She felt nothing at all when she stood before the stone—no guilt, no resentment, no sorrow. A part of her life was finished. Her future was unshadowed by the past. She left flowers at the grave and walked away. She would never return.

Epilogue

March 5, 1961

Thea Elizabeth Demeray was born on the first Sunday in March, a mild, sunny day, promising an early spring. Rynna had an easy labor, less than six hours altogether, and Ted was with her the whole time. The baby cried lustily at once, exercising her strong lungs. She weighed seven pounds, much smaller than Robert, but she was healthy, perfectly formed, and quite beautiful. She had only a little hair, fine and very blonde. She didn't have a cleft in her chin, but something in the shape of her head and the color of her clear, blue eyes reminded Rynna of Ted. She was unmistakably her father's child.

Signs of spring were everywhere. In her hospital room, Rynna lay surrounded by dozens of daffodils and lilies, which Ted had been unable to resist. Early morning sunlight flooded the room. She was so happy, lightheaded with relief and joy. A beautiful baby, a sweet little girl, a sister for Robert. What could be better?

Ted was sitting beside the bed in his wheelchair, and he looked much the way she felt. He hadn't said much, but he was clearly elated.

"When can we go home?" she asked.

"I'll ask the doctor," he said, but made no move to leave her.

A nurse came in, carrying a small, precious bundle. "Here's our little girl," she said. She would've given her to her mother, but Rynna gestured toward Ted, and the nurse laid the baby in his arms.

She was wrapped in a yellow blanket, as springlike as her silky flaxen hair. She gazed gravely up at her father, pursed her lips, and waved a tiny fist.

"She's beautiful," he whispered. He had tears in his eyes. "I don't want you to think I'll love her more than Rob," he said. "I couldn't."

"I know," Rynna assured him. She did know. She understood what acknowledging Jason's claim meant to him. He had made a sacrifice for her and for their son.

Thea yawned.

"That's right," Ted said. "Go to sleep. You're safe."

Spring would come. The future held only promise.

A word about the author...

Linda Griffin retired as Fiction Librarian for the San Diego Public Library to spend more time on her writing, and her work has been published in numerous journals.

In addition to the three Rs—reading, writing, and research—she enjoys Scrabble, movies, and travel.

Beyond Stonebridge is her ninth book from The Wild Rose Press, Inc.

http://www.lindagriffinauthor.com/